3:15 am and other stories.

Rudo D M Manyere

First published in Great Britain in 2022 by:

Carnelian Heart Publishing Ltd
Suite A
82 James Carter Road
Mildenhall
Suffolk
IP28 7DE
UK

www.carnelianheartpublishing.co.uk

Paperback ISBN	978-1-914287-25-1
Hardback ISBN	978-1-914287-26-8

A CIP catalogue record for this book is available from the British Library.

This collection of short stories is entirely a work of fiction. The names, characters and incidents portrayed in it are the work of the author's imagination. Any resemblance to actual persons, living or dead, is purely coincidental.

Editors:
Samantha Rumbidzai Vazhure
Lazarus Panashe Nyagwambo
Daniel Mutendi

Cover design & Layout:
Daniel Mutendi

Typeset by Carnelian Heart Publishing Ltd
Layout and formatting by DanTs Media

Contents

REVIEWS for 3.15AM and other short stories

A kaleidoscopic collection of short stories exploring themes close to Rudo Manyere's heart. Set in Zimbabwe, a motley of carefully crafted characters journey with you through a beautifully executed debut by a gripping new voice.

Samantha Rumbidzai Vazhure - Author & Poet, United Kingdom

Rudo sweeps the dark corners of history in gentle, simple strokes and out comes the dirt, the ugliness, the dust of human shortcomings and amidst them, the forgotten pennies and marbles, the love, the hope, the determination of human spirit.

Lazarus Panashe Nyagwambo - Author, Zimbabwe

Pick on any emotion: disillusionment, relief, grief, shock, guilt, shame, disgust, elation, the list goes on - Rudo Manyere can take you through these in just a paragraph. A powerful collection of short stories that touch on the lives of Zimbabweans, stretching from the colonial era through independence, to the turbulent times that followed. Fasten your seatbelts and prepare for a rollercoaster ride.

Daniel Mutendi - Author, Zimbabwe

Dear thirteen-year-old Rudo,

the fuel behind my love for literature

I hope I have made you proud.

For you, dear Reader

I hope this gives you the courage to write the book you want to read.

"… insist upon your right to go off on a tangent. Your right to put the spanner in the works. Your right to refuse to be labelled and to insist on your right to behave like anything other than what anyone else expects…"

-Dambudzo Marechera.

Kurauone

Previously published in
Brilliance Of Hope - an anthology of short stories compiled and edited by Samantha Vazhure.

Waiting outside WHSmith next to a dilapidated structure that used to be a beauty salon, I see Adesua, Kola's sister, standing across the street. She is hard to miss, with her afro regally crowning her head. The olive-green pin-stripe blouse and the black pencil skirt trace every inch of her curvaceous body and make her look *almost* professional. However, if I am being honest, the print of her curvaceous hips takes me back to the yester years when the three of us roamed around the streets of Oxford after our service to the city, as cleaners at St Margaret's College. She has not seen me yet, so I am standing here and taking her in. She has aged, she has webs of wrinkles around her eyes and instead of the strides she used to rhythm her walk to, she now has the gait of a pensioner. The green handbag and black pumps with a green flower she is wearing give a youthful touch to her outfit. The earrings carved with the African continent, which I bought for her from this Zimbabwean lady who charged me sixty pounds because they had been handmade and crafted, shipped and "escaped" customs, all the way from Zakarinopisa in Masvingo, complimented the outfit. They still turned heads, the earrings, the nose, chin and back head of the continent holding on to the corners of each earring.

Even after thirty odd years since our liaison came to an end, she still makes my heart flutter under my chest. I examine my posture and choice of attire on the large windows of the bookshop. My beard seems to "connect" as the youth say. I stroke it and as much as I am aware, I am still surprised by how white it has become. I only turned sixty-three last week and even though the lines on my face portray wisdom beyond my years, I am still holding on to the intensity of my boyish charm. My tucked in striped shirt and suspended trousers now make me look ridiculous, as my big *bele* pokes out, stretching my suspenders to my sides. The overcoat which I am beginning to regret because the heat is giving me vertigo, drapes on my shoulders as if it has been hung on. I ignore the sensation and firm my feet which are sheltered by my only pair of formal shoes. I lean on the window and take a minute to collect myself. I am not going to let my anatomy fail me now, not today and especially not in the presence of Adesua. I shake the feeling off and lean on the window. I wave at Susu, that is the sobriquet I had given her. She is standing on the other side of the street obviously searching for my face in the crowd.

"Susu!" I shout her name walking towards her, but with the earphones plugged in her ears, she obviously cannot hear me. I get closer to her and tap her shoulder. The smile that spreads on her face gives me nostalgia, the curl of her lip that reveals her white, carefully arranged dentition is deja vu of how she expressed her joy when I told her I loved her. Her love language was words of affirmation, and I hope it still is. " Kura!" She pronounces the first part of my name in her strong Yoruba accent. The "*ra*" part comes out like the roar of a lion cub. I do not care; I love the way she says it. I have always loved it. She reaches out for me and I embrace her. She stands on her toes and as much as I am tempted to lift and spin her around like before, I know my back will fail me. I linger and take in the smell of her hair which masks my face. It smells familiar, like the hair conditioner one of my housemates, the Kenyan lady, uses for her hair. Kanto, Kanu or Kanyu, I do not remember. She takes a deep breath and pulls back. I look at her and she tries to look away. I touch her shoulder and keep my hand there; she sniffles and places her hand on top of mine.

"It was unexpected. Too soon, j-just like that he did not wake up shaa." My Susu says as she digs for a piece of tissue in her bag. I search my overcoat for my handkerchief and hand it over to her. I smile as a wave of nostalgia hits me again, how we used to argue as to whether the "word" s*haa* was a Nigerian or Zimbabwean colloquial. "I know, he was in great health and had so much to live for." I reply, reminiscing about Kola, her brother, my best friend and the glue between us, who last week had died in his sleep. We stand by the street for a few minutes, ignoring the shoulders that nudge us and the clamour that surrounds us. "Come." I whisper, reaching for her hand, "If we get on the bus now, we will get there before a lot of people arrive. We can catch up for old times' sake." She looks at me and forces a smile, I do the same. We walk through Cornmarket Street on to St. Aldates and wait at bus stop 4T. Bus number 5 to Blackbird Leys will take us to the Community Hall where mourners will congregate and discuss how to raise money to send Kola's body back to Nigeria.

We sit in our designated seats, for elderly and disabled people. I look at Susu and laugh. She looks at me, confused, pursing her lips. "Do you remember that day when we were coming from reporting, from uhm, ah Eaton House in Hounslow and we swore we would never be caught dead sitting in these seats because in our forties we would be out of this country and living in a villa in France?" I continue to laugh, with a mixture of glee and disappointment. Forty years ago, we both were undocumented immigrants, in love and invincible. The Zimbabwean government had failed dismally and in West Africa, Nigeria was facing the same situation. A multitude of us had run away looking for greener pastures. I remember the time I had left Zimbabwe; I had been a trillionaire and had marched at more than fifteen rallies by the age of eighteen. Kola and Adesua used to laugh at me when I told them, they could not believe that a whole nation once accommodated trillionaires, but no one was rich. They began to call me Mr Trilionare Sir. With their thick accents, the "sir" was pronounced as "sar".

"Ah, we were so young and naive. If only we had known life would take us here, I would have stayed in Nigeria and Kola would still be alive and I w..."

"And you would have never met me." I murmur, looking out the window, hurt. I understand where she is coming from, but I cannot imagine her thinking of a world where we never existed. Kura and Susu. Kurauone and Adesua. The Zimbabwean and Nigerian couple. The Shona and Yoruba duo. A concoction by the African gods deemed good and pleasant in a foreign land.

"Kura, you know what I mean. I just cannot believe I, we, wasted most of our lives hoping and praying for something that was not meant for us." My Susu is saying this looking down, she cannot say it straight to my face because she knows it is not entirely true. We did not waste time; our love was not a waste of time.

"Susu, I know what you mean, and you know what I mean too. It so happens over the last years, I have had time to think. Not being documented for over thirty years will do that to you." I am telling her this and my heart is drumming in my chest. I understand the timing might be off, insensitive even, but I do not want to die the way Kola did. He only got his papers six months ago after battling the Home Office for as long as I have. He died in his sleep from exhaustion. The marathon shifts he took working as a health care assistant also known as BBC - British Bum Cleaner - had caught up with him. You would think at sixty-three he would be getting ready to retire, but just a year from retirement that is when he started working full time as a "legal" person. Just like me, he had taken small jobs here and there, which was and still is illegal, but it was the only way to survive.

He is survived by two daughters. Oladayo who he last saw when he left Nigeria; she was only two years old and after forty years, she would see her father again, this time in a coffin. Adenike was the daughter he begot with Alina, the Romanian lady he had succeeded in getting pregnant but not her papers. He had proposed I take the same route, get a lady from the EU or even better, an English woman. Get her pregnant and stick around long enough until they include you on their papers, and just like that you are a British citizen. "*Gwam gwam*, just like that my broda you are in. This United Kingdom will be yours for the taking in Jesus' name!" he would say each time he tried to sway me into following his footsteps. I could not do it, I had Susu. She was the only one I wanted to be the mother of my future children and my only life partner. I would always remind him I was in love with his sister and would not disrespect her or myself like that.

"Kura, I like you, you are a fine man and I am grateful for the way you love my sister but my broda, love is only an illusion. Will love give you *paper*? Will love give you red passport? Eeh? You need to be wise, by all means necessary get your *paper* then worry about love later. Ok, even if you choose Adesua, how will you provide for*ha* eeh? Each day you are playing cops and robbers with the police and Home Office because you are working illegally. Is that life?" He would question me but never give me enough time to explain. Which was something that gnarled me about him, but I liked how practical he was. He was a man of action. The 007 amongst us who had a license to kill every obstacle in his own way. I had taken his advice once; we both ended up in prison and that was the last time I took his advice.

We had registered with an agency with fake ID's and documentation to get the jobs. The IDs almost looked original. Manish, the Indian guy from Cowley was behind the masterpieces, after the astounding recommendation from our fellow immigrant peers. I do not know how they noticed or if it was a routine check, but the day they called us for training, a SERCO van parked outside and four huge men came in and asked us to produce our IDs and scanned our fingerprints. Long story short, we were arrested together with four other women who were also using fake IDs. For two years, we shared a cell, not by choice but after my cellmate was released, the correctional officers at HM Prison Bullingdon where we were in remand before our transfer, put us in one cell. That chapter of our lives frayed and strengthened our friendship. After serving our sentences, we were sent to a detention centre awaiting our deportation. I will not lie, that place was worse than prison. Not knowing when you would get out was torturous and heartrending. I saw grown men, fit and able men, kill themselves in that place. It was like being caught between a rock and a hard place - living illegally in a country you would never be accepted or surviving in your own country where you were never certain where the next meal would come from. The former was more tantalising, but it had its own consequences. I too had begun flirting with suicide, on days when my immigration lawyer, funded by the government, would come, and advise me to leave and go back to my country because I had no further evidence. I would go back to my room and anticipate how long it would take for me to bleed out if I slit my wrists, clench my fists and stood under the shower. A bath would have been better, but that service is not available in detention centres. I know it was cowardice, but which other choice did I have? I had no family, no savings and no dignity left, only Susu. Susu was the one who kept me alive, gave me hope and gave me the will to live.

"You know, Adenike says she doesn't want to be called by her African name but prefers Denisa, her second name, because it is easier to pronounce." Susu ropes me back to reality as we pass Templar Square. I look at her and sigh, words have escaped me.

"Hhhmm, was Kola aware of this?" I engage in the conversation.

"Yes, he was. He was not very happy about it, but I told him what did he expect when she had no idea or had never been to Nigeria? She only knows of *oyibo* people as her friends and family."

"That is true. She has never been exposed to your culture."

"Well, now no one will *paster* her to use her Yoruba name now that he is gone."

"*Aika,* are you not the aunt? Do you not have a say?"

"*Tufiakwa,* God forbid! After what that *oyibo*woman said to me when she was at odds with my brother? No! They do not exist to me."

"Susu, you are better than this. Are you not the one who always said, our personal feelings about something do not give us permission to ignore God's feelings about it?"

"Nxaa, you know you ought to start calling me Adesua now." She is muttering this as we alight at Balfour Road. She knows I am right, but she will not admit it.

"But I love calling you that, you will always be my Susu. Even now as we are wrinkled up with aching backs, you are forever my Susu and y-."

"And I am a married woman. Remember Steve, he is still alive you know."

"Oh yes, him. Your husband. How is his rheumatism? You know, he never replied to me when I asked him how old he was when he wrote Leviticus. It still keeps me awake at night." I am jesting but I mean it. That man is and was still old even back then. He is only four years older than me but still, he wasn't and still is not good enough for my Sus-, for Adesua. If only I had been released sooner from that hellhole of a detention centre. If only I had not spent six years in that place, I could have married her, but she could not wait any longer. The Home Office had denied her appeal, she had nothing else to submit and she was at an impasse. I remember the night she called me, we had just finished our night prayers at the detention centre and I was on my way back to my room for a roll call. She sounded distant and absent-minded, we talked as usual about our day, our future and how strong our love was.

"I am getting married," she blurted out. At first, I thought she was teasing me, like the times she would say she was pregnant, then after a few minutes would say, "with blessings on blessings on blessings." I was waiting for her to say that, but she went on to say she had met him online and he just wanted someone to be with and have children with - two maximum, she said. She had no choice, this was her only chance, so she took it.

I still had three more years in the detention centre when she decided to marry Steve. She would still send me money and write me letters, but I never replied, and I gave the money to those who were being deported to start a new life back in their homelands. I was not going to have another man take care of me. When I was released, I never tried to contact her, even though I would stalk her Facebook handle every night after my shift. It was Kola who had told me she had miscarried three times, but Steve had remained by her side because he had fallen in love with her. Who wouldn't? I did not like how he called her by her full name, Adesua, he was not creative or thoughtful at all. Although I am grateful, he did not tread towards Susu or Sue, at least Ade or Sua would have been inspiring.

"You are impossible, you know," she says laughing." He is a good man, a good husband."

"But do you love him, the way you loved me?"

"Kurauone, we are married. So, it means there is love there."

"In the words of Toni Morrison, your favourite writer, love is or is not, there is no thin or thick love. So, is it there or not?"

I know I must tread lightly, but I must know. Yesterday I finally got my papers. I found them on my doorstep after coming from work. They were in a large khaki envelope carefully sealed with a signed delivery sticker on it. My name was printed across the envelope in big bold letters: **MR KURAUONE NHAMO**. After forty-one years of waiting, they finally decided to grant me papers, but was it worth it if I had nothing to account for? Only a year from retirement and here I was trying to win the love of my life back. She is the real reason I have been keeping on and her reply will determine my future.

"We are moving. To France. Steve bought a villa in Lyon and we are retiring and moving there." She says, as we alight from the bus.

I feel like my soul has been punched out of my body.

My ears are ringing and that vertigo feeling is coming back hard and fast. She is living our dream with another man, that man is living my life. I stop in my tracks and look at her, I can feel the brim of my eyes burning but I will not succumb to it. My dotage catches up with me as I balance myself on a pole on the side of the road. I do not look at her, but I laugh out loud looking at the community hall on the other side of the street. She looks at me confused and I look at her pitiful and ashamed of myself. So, this is how it ends? It is either death by work or death by heartbreak. At sixty-three years old, I am standing next to a woman I have loved and chosen over myself every time, but she is here choosing herself all over again. I look at her laughing, then cup her face in my hands. I lean towards her and without a doubt in my soul, I whisper in her ear.

"I am going back to Zimbabwe."

At the end of the month

Since I was a child, my father took me everywhere with him. When I was six, he took me to his workplace at the end of the month when he went to collect his paycheque. He would open the envelope and make me read it to him. At the age of six, I was too young to understand. I always thought it was his way of helping me perfect my A B C's and 1 2 3's. Afterwards, he would lift me on his shoulders and we would walk around Harare whilst I ate some ice cream.

We would pass through Huruyadzo, the local bottle store, on our way home and he would buy a couple of pints of Black Label for himself and a Ripe 'n' Ready with Zapnax for me, and we would head home. He would lift me from his shoulders and set me on the single bed we shared. My father would turn on the Primus stove and I would light the candle and start working on my homework. Most times I would not be doing my homework, but I would stare at the pages in the dim light, waiting for baba to tell me a story. He always did whilst the sadza simmered, especially after downing one or two pints of his beer.

Ever since mama left, it had become our ritual. He brought out his book and sat in front of me. He called the book, "The book of life" and he only allowed me to touch it on these end-of-the-month special occasions. He would take a few sips and his bloodshot eyes gawked at me as I pretended to scribble in my homework book.

"We are royalty," he would start, "sons and daughters of great kings and queens." I would sit up straight and pay attention. I always loved his stories, how he made them seem real and how he actually believed them to be true. It always fascinated my young mind how he narrated the story as if he had experienced it.

"My great grandfather was still a young man when they came. Changamire Dombo was still the chief and he ruled with an iron fist," he would exclaim, raising his fisted hand in the air. "His name was Musorowegomo, my great grandfather. He was a great wrestler, and he was the best in the whole of the Rozvi State. The young women admired him and the young men wanted to be him." Baba would then take a swig from the bottle and wipe his mouth with the back of his hand. "He was sharpening his spear when they came. He heard people screaming and saw huts being set ablaze. People were running but they all fell when the *paa paa* noise sounded. It is said it came from the long sticks the men without knees were holding."

"Men without knees? How were they chasing them baba?"

"No, my boy," he would laugh, ruffling my head. "Back in the day, many years ago, our people were not familiar with the white men's clothes. They were not accustomed to clothing that went past the knees, so they called them 'men without knees' before they were called *varungu*."

"Ok baba." I would respond, settling in my chair.

"Where was I? Ah, yes. The men without knees rounded the people who were left and killed them, but my great grandfather survived. I do not know how he did it or how he convinced the white men, but he ended up being a servant and learnt to read and write." Baba would look at the book and flip through the pages. "This is the book that has our history. The book he wrote, and it has been passed down from generation to generation."

"Can you read it to me, baba?" He had never read the book to me. He only took it out and flipped through the pages and after telling me the story, which I had come to know by heart but still loved to hear anyway, he would place it in the shoebox where he used to keep his valuables, including my birth certificate and the single picture of my mother.

"Well son, it is because I cannot read," he would respond.

"But I can teach you, baba. I can now count to fifty and I know my a-e-i-o-u now."

"Haha, that's my clever boy." He would take another swig and look at me. "This is why I teach you to read and write. So, one day, you will read this out to me and I can get to know more about my forefathers and where I come from."

"Yes baba, I will read it to you every day when I grow up."

"Good boy. Now, take out the plates so I can serve dinner."

"Yes, baba."

1965

Vongai glanced at her wristwatch and sighed as she waited for Nurse Margaret to release her. It was 5:47 pm and from her calculations, it would take her twenty minutes to walk from St Andrew's Fleming Hospital to the bus stop. She knew she was going to be late leaving the city centre and already being on her second warning did not bring her any comfort. Ever since Ian Smith announced the Unilateral Declaration of Independence (UDI), a statement adopted by the Cabinet of Rhodesia in November 1965, announcing that Rhodesia would no longer be under the British government's rule and would be solely ruled by the white minority, life for the blacks in Rhodesia had gone from bad to worse.

The United Kingdom, the Commonwealth and the United Nations had all deemed the UDI illegal. However, Rhodesia had still broken away and continued as an unrecognised state with the assistance of South Africa and Portugal. The UDI system promoted segregation and discrimination with unfair regulations such as: blacks were not allowed to be in the City Centre past 6 pm; blacks needed to have separate restrooms and modes of transport; the only brand of alcohol that blacks were allowed to drink was *Chibuku* and blacks were only exposed to limited education. Vongai had only qualified to get the job as a nurse at St Andrew's Fleming because her grandfather had been a missionary who had helped convert myriads of African people. She had an opportunity most black people in Rhodesia could only dream of, which was partly why she never complained. Still, Nurse Margaret and all the other white nurses made sure she knew what she was and always would be – a kaffir.

Vongai walked towards the entrance to see if Nurse Margaret was on her way to take over for the night shift. She saw Nurse Margaret a short distance from the entrance to the hospital, leaning against the wall, lighting a cigarette. Vongai was not surprised by her actions. Nurse Margaret had overtly expressed that she did not like black people and saw them as inferior. Expecting her to be concerned about her safety would be silly and naive. Vongai sighed. She felt fear and uncertainty as she contemplated whether to go to Nurse Margaret or wait for her to come and release her. Waiting would mean she would have to walk all the way from the hospital to Mufakose where she lived. Going to the nurse would mean starting a war she would never win. She resolved to stand by the door and wait for her.

"Vongai!" Nurse Margaret barked as she walked towards Vongai who was removing her stockings behind the reception area, preparing for the long walk home. There would be no mode of transport for black people and the only safe – well, relatively safer way was to walk the ten miles home. "Vongai!" Nurse Margaret called again, her voice husky and loud. At fifty-six, she looked older than her age. Her hanging skin quivered with every expression and the way she drew her eyebrows made her look animated and angry. "Go on now. Won't you be late catching your bus just standing there?" Vongai hurriedly went out the door, afraid of the journey ahead more than Nurse Margaret's rants.

Being a black person walking in the city after 6 pm was dangerous in Rhodesia but being a twenty-five-year-old black woman walking alone after 6 pm was deadly. If anything were to happen to her, no-one would come to her aid. The law clearly stated: **NO KAFFIRS IN THE CITY AREA AFTER 6PM.** Vongai quickened towards the black designated bus stop which was in the same direction as her secret route.

There was not a soul in sight as she half ran and half walked home, only the chirping of crickets and her thoughts to keep her company. She prayed Tungamirai would be waiting for her at the bus stop or, fingers crossed, he would walk towards the city to meet her halfway. If that was the case, she knew he would take the route they had chosen to use if an incident like this took place. Tunga had suggested they use the route after many black people had been imprisoned or killed after using the main road from the city after 6 pm. He always worried about her. After all, he had vowed to love and protect her till death.

Pacing through the dusty pathway which was covered with shrubs and long stems of grass, Vongai thought of the one-bedroom house she owned with Tunga. He had just finished painting their kitchen walls and the smell sickened her, but she still looked forward to being there because it was her home. Having lived with four brothers and three sisters, sharing a house with one person was heaven on earth. With Tunga, she no longer had to time herself when having a bath or just looking at herself in the bathroom mirror. These small pleasures made her long for home on her long day shifts at the hospital.

She increased her pace when she saw the lights from the Bakayawa Grocery Store. They indicated that she was half-way home and she was at least safe from the white patrols, but still a target for the local robbers. At least her own kind would only harass and steal from her; they would not beat her to a pulp. Vongai thought of her future and of bringing children into a world where their future was determined by the colour of their skin, a world where you could never be yourself before you were told who you were supposed to be. She had had this discussion with Tunga and numerous times he had threatened to send her back to her father's house. She wished he understood her perspective. The pain she went through each day at work and the life they lived did not feel like the one that God had intended for either of them.

"Please, I do not want to hear about this nonsense. *Wazvinzwa*? Do you hear me? I want children. All my friends have children and now they think you are infertile or I am impotent," Tunga had said the last time they had talked about it. She remembered how he had been holding a half stab of cigarette, leaning forward in his chair as he sat opposite her.

He always furrowed his eyebrows when he was upset and would not look at her. Vongai stood up and went to the kitchen. She stood by the empty sink where Tunga had washed the dishes earlier that day. He was a good husband and never made her feel less than himself. Yet that would never be enough to have her bring a child into such a hateful and painful world. She took a glass from the rack, poured water into it, then left it on the sink, untouched. She walked towards the living room which also doubled as the dining room and bid goodnight to Tunga. He grunted his response as he slammed their twenty-one-inch black and white television to adjust the volume.

***

"Where is Fungai?" Tunga asked, putting his pint down. "I thought he was coming to join us tonight *wani.*" He gestured at Gumi to pass him the lighter he held in his hand and then sat beside Chenjerai who was getting comfortable in his seat.

"*Ah iwe,* you should know never to make plans with a man who has just got married." Gumi blew some cigarette smoke in the air and they all laughed.

"Knowing Fungai, I am pretty sure the wife is already pregnant. You remember how quickly his first wife got pregnant? First week of marriage!"

"Only to find out the child was not his," Chenjerai said passively and the three men all laughed again, the sound filling the dingy shebeen. It was owned by Tom Brown, the only white person who had willingly chosen to live amongst the blacks in Mufakose. He had been threatened several times by the UDI police to leave the town and live amongst his own kind. At one point, he had been offered a two-bedroom house and a pub in the Highlands area that was predominantly white. The condition, however, was he would have had to leave everything behind, including his wife, Natsai and their three coloured children. He refused to move nor did he even consider the "option". To him, love was a right, not a possibility.

Not everyone thought it wise however, especially the black men of Mufakose who always reminded him what a grave mistake he had made. They thought he was stupid for not taking the opportunity to leave the slums and have a proper and decent life. Some even thought he was mocking them by turning the government down, making it seem as if it was bearable and easy to be a black person in Rhodesia. He had tried to explain overtly, numerous times, that his views were not the same as other white people's. He believed in equality and mutual respect and did not expect to be treated differently because he was white. The men would all scoff, some shaking their heads and others laughing. "Equal and mutual respect? Is this man alright upstairs? He thinks it's fun for us to only be limited to being garden boys and builders regardless of how intelligent we are?" Each one would take away something different from what he said, but none of them ever considered that he meant it.

Tom walked over to the corner at the back of the shebeen where the three men were lounging with a quarter bottle of Springbank and shot glasses. There was a small round table that looked like it had been handed down several generations before it found itself in the shebeen, a brown double sofa with tattered arm rests where Tunga and Chenjerai sat and three bar stools that circled the small table. The low roof made Gumi hunch as he stood near the window, putting his cigarette out. The three men saw Tom walking towards them and exchanged glances.

"Look, your friend has brought a peace offering for the pain his people are causing us," Chenjerai whispered to Tunga who was nursing his second pint of *Chibuku*.

"Ah, leave him be. He is trying to be friendly, give him a break," Tunga rebuked him.

"Hey, be nice to him. He has whiskey and it's been a while so, Chenjerai do not spoil this for me. We do not need to hear how as a black man you are oppressed and can only use one ply tissue paper," Gumi whispered, picking up a bar stool and moving next to the sofa.

"One ply? *Sha*, that is a luxury. Why do you think I always collect newspapers here? Just put a bit of water for them to soften and they are as good as three-ply tissue."

They all burst out laughing. As if on cue, Tom approached them and sat on one of the stools, smiling at them.

"Gentlemen, *maswera sei*? Good evening." Tom greeted them, setting the bottle of Springbank and the four shot glasses on the table which was stained with ashes and streaks of beer. *My girl* by The Temptations was playing for the umpteenth time since the shebeen had opened. It had just been released and RBC FM was making sure everyone knew the lyrics by the time they went to bed.

"*Mudhara* Tom, how are you this evening?" the men chorused. Gumi turned his attention to the bottle of brownish-gold liquor that was calling his name. Chenjerai excused himself and went to the restroom. Gumi had never been a fan of the cheap and uninspired brand of alcohol that the blacks were restricted to. His taste buds had savoured quality alcohol from the time he had worked for Mr. Walker – who sold diluted whiskey and spirits to "upper-class" black people. Gumi was known all over Mufakose for his fine taste in quality alcohol and cigarettes. It was mostly because ninety percent of the time, he was the one that made them. He studied the colour of the liquor and he could tell, by the way the light from the bulb over them pierced the bottle, that it was diluted. He conceded that diluted whiskey was better than the *Chibuku* that was causing him to gain weight. Gumi lit another cigarette and paid attention to Tom who was mid-sentence, talking to the other two gentlemen whom he was certain were eager to have a shot too.

"...business has been good. Terrific even. My father-in-law has agreed to help me open another shebeen at his house in the meantime." Tom said as he stared at his wife, Natsai, who was behind the counter, taking orders from drunk and semi-drunk customers. Tunga saw him looking at his wife and instantly thought of Vongai. He did not understand why Tom suddenly took time to glance at his wife mid conversation, but he liked it and he could not help but miss his own. Tom saw Tunga looking at him and turned to him.

"She is beautiful, isn't she?" Tom said to Tunga who was trying to pretend as if he had not been looking at him.

"Yes." Tunga nodded his head and took a sip of his *Chibuku*, wishing it was whiskey.

"You know, it was love at first sight for me. I just knew she would be my wife the first time I saw her at her mother's market," Tom reminisced. Gumi and Chenjerai, who had now joined them, listened reluctantly.

"She was not even paying attention to me. I was overseeing the men who were constructing my father's bar and I would walk past her market countless times a day." Tom chuckled to himself. The three men were a little uncomfortable with the white man's need to confide in them. They had known him from the time he came to Mufakose six years ago, exchanging pleasantries and congregating around the small stereo when there was a soccer match. However, they had not been acquainted enough to borrow cigarettes from him or know if he had any siblings, yet here he was, baring his heart and telling them his love story.

"So, *mudhara*, how did you end up 'conquering' the situation?" Chenjerai insinuated, shuffling in his seat next to Tunga who understood his pun. All four of them knew where the conversation was headed. Tom reached for the bottle of whiskey and poured into the shot glasses. He gestured for the men to each take one before they all toasted and gulped down their shots.

There followed an awkward silence for a few seconds. Gumi complimented the fine and exquisite texture of the whiskey. Tunga agreed with him through grunts and hand gestures. Anything to fill the loud silence was welcome. They knew Chenjerai would not let it go though. He had been orphaned after his parents were burnt alive in their house after they declined an offer to sell their farm for a price less than the cost of a single cow. He had ended up living with his grandmother in the reserves. He had never been able to see white people as genuine and considerate people. He was not afraid to show that he had been hurt and he made it no secret. He was not violent or menacing although he asked questions that would have people, both black and white, question themselves.

Chenjerai sat quietly, observing the men around him. He turned his gaze to Tom who was looking at him, about to say something. He thought of interrupting him but decided to let him proceed.

"I did not 'conquer' anything, nor did I threaten her. I was respectful of her space and I knew the danger she would be in if she were to even talk to me. I just watched her from a distance for nine months and on Sundays, on her way to church." Tom shuffled himself on the three-legged stool.

Falling in love with Natsai was the only decision Tom was proud of and he felt he was privileged to have been loved back by her. She was the most beautiful woman he had ever seen when he first saw her those six years ago. She was twenty-one years old, ambitious, independent and fearless. Her parents were worried that she was getting a bit too old and no one would find her suitable or attractive if she did not get married soon. She had told them that marriage was not something she was worried about and what was important to her was her teaching career. As an only child, this did not go down well with her parents, especially her mother who began holding prayer meetings with *madzimai eruwadzano* every Thursday to drive out the spirit that had possessed her daughter.

Tom learnt about this when he was eavesdropping on one of the conversations the builders had during their break. One of them lived in the same neighbourhood as Natsai. This particular builder had tried to pursue her, but like the rest of the other men before him, he had found her intimidating and intolerant of his juvenile pursuits.

Tom had tricked his sister, Kathleen, who was a senior teacher at the school Natsai was hoping to be employed, to hire female black teachers. He had convinced her by suggesting that by hiring a black teacher, the school would portray a more 'diverse' spectrum and it would make her look good when the Pope and priests visited the school. He knew Kathleen was not keen on associating herself with kaffirs, but impressing the Catholic board was as important as entering heaven to her. He did not care about using his sister's racist nature against her, caring only that he would see Natsai up close, without her getting into trouble. He stole glances at Natsai every time he dropped by to see Kathleen.

His tall frame, broad shoulders, blonde frizzy hair and blue eyes did not go unnoticed by the other ladies at the school. Hillary, Kathleen's deputy, tried throwing herself onto him whenever she got the chance, but Tom always came up with an excuse to avoid going out with her. He eventually agreed after learning that Natsai was being supervised by Hillary. Because of that, he agreed to meet up with Hillary at the school, on the condition that there was someone else as a witness. When Hillary pondered on who to ask, he readily suggested Natsai whom he knew would have no choice since she had to follow Hillary everywhere. Hillary could not refuse, already being twenty-four and desperate, and because the other female teachers envied her for having been chosen by Tom.

Every weekday during Hillary's break, Tom went to the school and they all sat on the terraces at the sports field. Natsai would sit at a distance, but Tom made sure to include her in the conversation and most of the time, he talked to her more than Hillary. Natsai did not seem interested nor did she pay much attention to him during their encounters.

One day, Hillary became annoyed because Natsai was laughing at one of Tom's jokes and she reached out and slapped Natsai. Tom was baffled and angered by her reaction. He quickly ran to Natsai and held her face. He felt the warmth of the single tear streak running down her smooth, black cheek. He gazed into her dark brown eyes which changed to a light brown when she faced the sun. Tom looked at her for a while. He could not believe anyone could be more beautiful. Natsai pulled away from him and briskly walked towards the classrooms, not turning back.

"Oh Tom, why do you care?" Hillary snapped at him. She made her way towards him, tucking a few strands of brown locks behind her ear. "These people get too comfortable and before you know it, they start asking you for money." She put her arms around Tom's neck and searched his eyes as he looked down. She kissed him on the lips, but he did not respond. When she tried using her tongue, Tom pushed her back and looked at her.

"That is no way to treat a human being! You should be ashamed of yourself. How can you think someone is less than you based on the colour of their skin?" Tom exclaimed, moving away from her. Hillary was confused. She had not expected him to react that way. *Why should she be ashamed of herself? She was not the one who was wrong. That woman should have known her place and kept quiet. Why did she have to apologise?* Hillary questioned herself as she watched Tom running towards the classrooms. She began running after him, calling his name.

Tom stopped and waited for her to catch up. He turned around and looked at her and saw that she appeared more confused than remorseful. "You had no right to hit her." He shook his head. "She did not deserve that. And a word to the wise Miss Kent, *these* people are as human as you are. They reason, they love and they hurt just like you!" He walked away from her and went to the staff room.

The room was empty and he did not know where to find Natsai. He did not even attempt to ask, afraid it would raise questions and it would get her in trouble. Tom walked to his truck and drove away nursing anger and a broken heart. He thought he would never see Natsai again. It was not until a year later that he met her at another school across town where she was a standard three teacher. He was foreseeing the building of an additional block at the school. That time around, he made sure to be intentional and brave, and the rest was history.

***

Tom poured another round of whiskey after narrating his love story. Chenjerai, Gumi and Tunga took some time to digest the story, trying to find the lesson or the takeaway from it. Tom took his shot and cleared his throat then looked at the three men who now looked tired.

"Chenjerai, I might not have answered your question, but I hope you see that for me, being with Natsai is more than any house they can give me. I saw a black woman who I fell hopelessly in love with and I could not have been happier." He grinned at Natsai who was clearing the counter, readying to close up. "*Akandipa* three amazing children and she loves me dearly. We love each other and I am a blessed man. Love knows no colour and when you find it, never let it go. It is a once in a lifetime kind of thing. It is not easy, but it is worth it." Tom stood up when he saw Natsai walking towards them to dismiss the remaining customers.

"Alright, alright, I am sure your wives are waiting? It is past 10 pm and I am sure they are worried sick," she joked, smiling at the three men who stood up as she approached.

"Ah *sisi* Natsai, blame *mudhara* Tom here. He is the one who kept us here for so long." Chenjerai said, stretching himself and walking towards the door with Gumi and Tunga behind him. They all laughed as they walked out, bid their farewells and left Tom and Natsai in the shebeen.

They walked towards *Chigubhu Road* where they all resided, separated only by a few houses. They had grown up on that street and had been friends ever since primary school.

They walked in silence, each pondering Tom's story. Was he just telling them or were they to take something from it?

Chenjerai decided to break the silence. "Ah but *varume*, what was the point of *mudhara* Tom's story? Huh? Was it to show us that his wife loves him more than the other wives love their husbands?" He was exasperated. He was still single and had vowed not to marry until the country was free from Smith and his men. This did not seem to be happening anytime soon.

"No *kani*, I think he was just sharing his experience. He is a man in love and is not afraid to show it. He makes me want to make it official with Shuvai, but that one is a wild card. You know she wears trousers? My mother will die if I bring her home." It was Gumi contemplating marrying the one woman who challenged him and drank as much as him.

"I think he was trying to say love knows no colour. He married someone who was not deemed to be good enough by anyone or worthy by his own kind, but he chose love. Love is like a tree; it grows wherever it wants. I guess he was trying to emphasise loving whoever you want regardless of what people say," Tunga gave his two cents as he too tried to dissect Tom's story.

"Ah, I hope he was not trying to mellow us into ignoring what his people are doing to us. I will not be tricked. Ah *kana*, no. I will not succumb to that." Chenjerai protested. He walked towards his small, one-room wooden cottage. He bade his friends goodnight and disappeared into the room. Gumi and Tunga proceeded to their homes which were a few houses down.

"You know, I get what *mudhara* Tom was on about. He is not like the rest of them but *shaa*, that does not excuse how we are treated like dogs. Their dogs have better lives than we will ever have." Gumi kissed his teeth and shook his head. It was hard to have faith or hope for a better life. He imagined how bringing children into this world would be setting them up for failure. Their lives would be limited and agonising.

Tunga shook his head but did not say anything. He agreed and understood his friend. He thought about how Vongai had tried to explain to him how raising a black child in Rhodesia was a permanent life sentence, full of pain, poverty and condescension. He did not want anyone to suffer like that and he did not want to partake in bringing into the world an innocent soul, to be castrated before they learnt who they were for themselves. He had to make peace with the possibility that he might never father a child. He parted ways with Gumi and headed towards his house. A few houses still had their lamps on. He could hear a few voices from people who were putting out their cooking fires and others filling buckets and drums with water, readying for the next morning.

As he approached their house, he saw that the lamp was on. Usually, Vongai would not have waited for him because she always had to get up before 5 am. He paced towards the house, worried Vongai had forgotten to turn the lamp off. When he got into the house, he saw Vongai sitting on the sofa, a large basket in front of her on their small coffee table. She sat stone-faced and teary, staring at the basket.

“Why are you seated by yourself this late?” Tunga inquired as he walked over to Vongai. He towered over both Vongai and the basket in their tiny living/dining room. Vongai looked at him but could not muster the courage to say anything. She began to cry and covered her face with her hands. Tunga knelt beside his wife and embraced her whilst she sobbed.

“Tell me *mudiwa*, what is it? Was it that horrid senior nurse again?” He tried to console his wife, kissing her forehead. He did not want to rush her. So, he held her and waited for her to compose herself. Vongai held her husband’s face and looked into his eyes. Tunga saw fear in hers and the first thing that came to his mind was someone had died, but he could not bring himself to ask her. Vongai looked at the basket and sighed.

“Tunga, I am sorry, but I could not leave it. I just could not!” She began sobbing again. “I know I could have just left it there and kept walking, but I could not.” Tunga realised she had walked home from work again, but that did not explain the basket. He looked at it. It looked ordinary, with a lid which had a knotted handle, but it was not familiar. He tried to think and guess what would make his wife that upset.

“Please, do not be angry. I know we will be in trouble but please, j–j…” She began to cry again, this time pointing at the basket. Tunga stood up and looked at the basket and braced himself. Could she be playing with him? She had done that a couple of times before. But this time she looked serious. He composed himself and opened the basket. He gasped, not believing what he was seeing. He looked at his wife, confused, trying to comprehend the meaning of what was in front of him. Where and how had she come across it? Had she stolen it from the hospital? She knew better than to steal anything; that much he knew. So, what was the meaning of this?

Tunga looked at Vongai who now stood beside him, looking into the basket too. He could not believe she would do this; create more strife for them whilst they could barely survive their current ones. They both looked at each other, lost for words, Vongai, still teary eyed and sniffling, Tunga, confused and now afraid, and the basket with its contents, snug and peaceful.

"Woman, explain to me why there is a whole baby with blonde hair and white skin in that basket?" Tunga slumped onto the seat Vongai had previously sat on, waiting for his wife to explain how she ended up with a white baby in the middle of Mufakose squatter camp in 1965.

***

"What do you mean you could not leave it there? You could have just walked away, and just left it there!" Tunga shouted at Vongai and pointed at the basket sitting on the sofa. Vongai had explained to him how she had heard an unusual sound whilst she was walking home from work. Nurse Margaret had delayed her again. This time she had asked her to stay a while longer so she could go to the south wing which was a fifteen-minute walk both ways, to borrow a cigarette from the other nurses.

"Tungamirai, *my love,* please hear me out," Vongai knelt next to him as she pleaded. She had relayed the incident numerous times, trying to convince Tunga how she could not have just walked away.

She was halfway home, a few minutes from Bakayawa Grocery Store, when she heard a strange noise near the big Msasa tree which marked the border to the Mufakose Township. She had thought little of it since she knew no robbers would be lurking that close to where people could see them. She ignored the noise and kept walking towards the township, but as she did so, she heard it again, a loud wailing from where the tree was. She could not see anyone. She began to think it was Peggy, the infamous phantom that had been known to roam around Mufakose, luring drunk men and late travellers to their misfortune. She stopped in her tracks, afraid, already beginning to think of how she was going to run if it were Peggy. Could she outrun a ghost? What if it was a *dzangaradzimu*? That would be worse because although they were known not to be violent, they used their height to scare you.

As she stood there, contemplating her fate, the wailing became louder and began to sound like a baby. Vongai snapped herself out of her thoughts and paid attention to where the crying was coming from. She began to walk back, listening attentively, trying to pick out where exactly the noise was coming from. From the dim light supplied by the moon, Vongai was able to make out a huge basket underneath the big Msasa tree. The noise appeared to be coming from the basket. As she got nearer to it, it sounded more like a new-born baby crying. She walked towards the basket and looked at it for a long time before deciding what to do. Was it truly a child or was she falling for a hoax? What if it was a *tokoloshi* or someone who was trying to lure her and murder her on the spot? As she was trying to make sense of it, the crying began again. The cry sounded husky and low, as if the baby was exhausted from crying. Without thinking twice, Vongai opened the basket and was shocked when she saw a baby, not more than three days old, partly swaddled in a white sheet, with no clothes underneath.

"*Mwari wangu*!" Vongai exclaimed, picking the baby from the basket. The sheet had come undone and the baby's tiny hands were out, its fists in its mouth. Vongai could not help but notice the baby was very pale. She thought maybe someone had abandoned the baby because it had albinism and they did not want to be shunned. However, as she fully unwrapped the baby, trying to see if it had a napkin, she noticed the straight blonde hair. She lifted the baby to her face to see clearly, unable to believe her eyes. *A white baby dumped close to the township? Why and who would do such a thing? Were they hoping someone would find the baby or they just wanted to get rid of it?* She instinctively began to rock the baby and wrapped "him" with her cardigan and stockings after removing the wet sheet. She did not have anything for him to eat, so she left him to his fists. He looked helpless and leaving him would be inhumane. *What would Tunga say?* She had made up her mind not to have kids and was adamant about it.

"What am I going to do?" she murmured to herself as she rocked the baby. He looked very peaceful and seemed to have fallen asleep.

"I cannot take you home. What will my husband say? I cannot leave you here either. What if you d..." Whilst she was contemplating what to do, she heard a ruffling in the bushes and a voice from where the pathway was. She carefully put the baby back in the basket. As she picked it to hide it in a tree hollow on the Msasa tree, she was startled by someone poking her with something blunt on her back.

"You kaffir. Wh...What are y...you doing here?" a male voice bellowed, poking her back. Vongai froze, terrified, when she recognised the voice. It was Sergeant Burke. He was a villainous and crude UDI officer. He was known for arresting black people for absurd things and was feared by everyone in the township except Mr Tom who was his brother-in-law. Vongai slowly turned around to face him, praying he would not harass her, but most of all, that he would not ask her to open the basket which she still held in her hand. She looked at the baton in his hand, the same one that had previously been used to poke her, and her heart sank. She had never been a victim of police brutality. Tunga had always made sure they avoided any encounters with the UDI police. But she had seen its sinister markings on her neighbours and family members.

"Answer me!" he bawled at her, staggering and struggling to stand still. Vongai was terrified. She thought of just pushing him out of her way and running for her life, but fear paralysed her.

"I…I was relieving m…myself sir," she lied, hoping he was going to be repulsed by her activity and leave her.

"Bloody hell, you people are disgusting! Animals!" he bellowed, standing in front of Vongai, gawking at her. Vongai stood there, scared for her life and hoping the baby would not make a sound.

"W…What do you have in there? O…open it, n…n…" Sergeant Burke moved towards her, pointing at the basket.

Vongai moved back, trying to distance herself from him. He kept moving forward, inching closer to her until she was pressed against the Msasa tree. She could smell the stale odour of alcohol and sweat on him. She was terrified and wanted to cry, but she also did not want to wake the baby. Sergeant Burke held on to the basket tightly with one hand and her chest with the other one. He moved closer to her and stared at her for a few seconds without saying anything. He glared at her chest and then her face and smiled. Vongai began to sob. She knew what he was thinking and knew what would follow. She thought of pushing him away, but she was afraid he had seen her face and would recognise her when he came to do his patrol rounds in Mufakose. Sergeant Burke slowly put his head on her chest, his arms hanging on both sides. Vongai stood there, paralysed. The baby was starting to whimper. She tried to sway the basket so the baby would not feel scared or alone, but it did not help. The baby began to cry very audibly. She could not move because of the

Sergeant's upper body weight on her chest. He was not moving or talking and the only sign of life was his breathing. She instantly realised he had fallen asleep on her chest. To free herself and attend to the crying baby, she pushed the sergeant off her chest. He slumped on the ground with a thud and let out a groan. He let out a few grunts then began to snore. Vongai ran for her life.

***

"*Ndamhanya*. I did not even stop at Mai Kaitano's shop for the bread and milk for tomorrow," Vongai said as she explained to her husband, still kneeling next to him. She went on to add how, when she arrived home, she had taken the baby out of the basket and bathed it. She saw that it was a boy and he had a big wound on his right leg. It made him wince every time she touched or moved his leg. Vongai had dressed the wound in some gauze and dressings that she had managed to get from the hospital one time when Tunga had been injured after the roof of one of the houses they were working on had collapsed whilst he was inside. She wrapped him in one of Tunga's t-shirts and cut two holes into her shower cap to make a homemade waterproof napkin.

"Has he eaten?" Tunga asked, leaning over to get a closer look at the baby. He felt sorry for him, but he still did not want to get attached either.

"Yes. I gave him the last of the fresh milk." Vongai took the baby who had begun to whimper out of the basket. She began to rock him, trying to soothe him. She checked the shower cap to see if he was wet, but it was dry. She felt tired and could not figure out why the baby was crying.

"I just fed him. I do not know why he is still crying. Shh shh. *Heehuwe chinyarara mwana. Heehuwe ch…chi…*" Vongai began to cry. She was scared and the shock of what she had done was beginning to sink in.

"Dear Lord, what have I done?" She sobbed as the baby wailed in her arms.

Tunga stood up and took the baby from Vongai. He did not want to say anything that would further upset her, even though he had a lot to say. *Fuck, Vongai so? She could have just easily walked away and not tried to pry. Now she is crying over something that could have been avoided. I guess this is for better or for worse, I just never imagined she would be the death of me.* Tunga thought these things to himself as he rocked the baby in one hand and held Vongai with the other.

"Go to sleep Vongai, you have work tomorrow. I will take care of him and think of a way forward." Tunga suggested, standing in the lounge-diner, rocking the baby who was turning red from crying. He was trying to find a way to calm him before their nosy neighbour came knocking.

"I do not mind staying up Tunga. I…I brought him here so…I should take care of him," Vongai replied, standing next to him. She was trying to collect herself and take on the burden she had added on to their already difficult life. She knew Tunga was already scheming on what to do next. He had always been the problem solver in the marriage and never one to point a finger. He unfailingly showed that they were a team.

"No, I will take care of him. Do not worry," he urged, walking to their kitchen unit which he had fashioned himself. He did not look at Vongai or show any emotion. He tried to rock the baby who was now crying with a rasp. He needed time to himself to figure out how they were going to go about their situation. He was furious, but he knew overtly expressing it in that moment would not lead to any resolution.

"Ok, goodnight. If you need anything, please wake me. There is a bit of mil…"

"Vongai, please, go to bed. I am a grown man and I can take care of a child, ok!" He blurted out whilst turning to face the kitchen unit, avoiding Vongai. His outburst startled the baby who had stopped crying and now started whimpering again. Vongai sighed and quietly walked out of the room. She knew saying anything would make Tunga angrier. She did not get the chance to have a wash before bed or perform her night-time skin care routine. She trod into their bedroom whose furniture consisted of a three-quarter bed, a washing basket, a wooden shoe rack with their two pairs of shoes each and a chest of drawers. The chest contained a can of Macho spray, a tub of Vaseline, a jar of Oil of Olay she had got from Nadia, a small bottle of Mum deodorant, a can of Kiwi shoe polish, face powder and two shades of lipstick. A *zambia* divided a quarter of the room to cover their clothes which were carefully arranged against the wall. She put on her nightdress and tied her hair. She stood in the middle of the room, trying to hear if the baby was still crying and to determine what Tunga was doing.

She checked the time on her wristwatch as she put it on the chest of drawers. It was a little past midnight and she would have to be up in four hours. She got under the covers and fluffed her pillow which was stuffed with old clothes and dried lavender. She held the blanket to her chin and tried to sleep.

After a while, she began to pray inaudibly. "*Mwari*, thank you for Tunga and for giving me the courage to save this baby. However, I do not know what to do now. Hear me Lord, what will I do? May this not backfire and may it not break my marriage, please. Please God, please. It is the only good thing in my life." Tears rolled down her face as she drifted off to sleep.

Tunga put on the Primus stove and placed the kettle on the plate, holding the baby in his free hand. The baby was wide awake, sucking his fists. Tunga tried to put him back in the basket, but he began to cry as soon as he put him down. He picked him up and he stopped crying. He put him down again and as soon as he did so, he began to cry again.

"What the hell! Is there something biting you in that basket?" Tunga asked, surveying the basket but unable to find anything. He could not understand why the baby was crying. He put him on the sofa and as soon as he laid him down, he began to wail loudly. Tunga quickly picked him up and he immediately stopped crying. He began to laugh, realising the baby did not want to be put down. It dawned on him that he must be feeling lonely and was scared to be left alone. Tunga moved him closer to the lamp and looked at him. The light pierced through the baby's blue eyes who remained concentrated on his fists.

"What shall we do with you, huh? You are clueless about how much trouble we are in, but it is not your fault," he whispered to the baby who was oblivious of what was going on. The kettle began to hiss on the Primus stove and Tunga rushed to turn it off, still holding the baby in his arms.

He could not find anything to use as a bottle for the baby, so he put the milk in a tumbler and placed it in a dish with hot water to warm the milk. He thought of how best he would feed him and then remembered they had an unused syringe which Vongai had brought from the hospital. He searched all the drawers in the kitchen and after a while, found it with the cutlery. He was not sure whether the baby would like or even take the plain milk, so he added a bit of sugar.

"After the day you have had, you deserve something sweet," Tunga said as he sat down with the tumbler of milk, the syringe and the baby. He tested the temperature of the milk on his arm and was satisfied that it was optimum before he drew some milk from the tumbler with the syringe. As soon as he put the syringe on the baby's lips, he began to suck on it frantically. Tunga pushed the syringe slowly to avoid choking him.

"What shall we do with you now?" He sighed deeply as he gave the baby the milk.

Tunga looked at him whilst he suckled on the syringe. What was he going to do? He could not leave it entirely to Vongai. He had always feared her good heart would put them in an uncomfortable situation. It was one of her many attributes that attracted him to her. She was always selfless and kind, yet firm. However, this time, it was Tunga who had to be the selfless and kind one. He was still in his infancy when it came to these qualities. All he knew was he had to protect his family, which was wholly comprised of Vongai and she was all he needed.

Upon realising that the baby had fallen asleep, Tunga carefully put him back in the basket. He stood up and looked at the baby, contemplating the plan he had quietly hatched whilst feeding him. He shook his head and walked towards the door. It was already dawn. The birds were singing their morning chorus and he could hear Dudzai, their neighbour, preparing her floor polish and soft brooms for her first round. She always started shouting from her yard and this would alert Vongai that it was time to wake up. Tunga braced himself for his wife to come into the dining room. He decided to tell her the plan he had come up with. It was the only way they would *all* be safe.

"There is nothing we can do now," he whispered to himself as he stood by the door. He took out a cigarette, rolled it between his fingers, then shrugged and put it on his lips and lit it. "That is the only way," he reiterated, thinking out loud and blowing the cigarette smoke towards Dudzai's house. Coincidentally, she started her marketing slogan.

"Cooooobraaaaa! Coooobraaaa! Cobra *ye*red, black *neeeye* white! Coooooobraaa! *Miiiiitsvairooo*!" she shouted as she walked down the road, oblivious to what was happening next door.

***

Tom rolled over and looked at Natsai who lay on her stomach, fast asleep, facing him. He studied her face. He never got tired of looking at it. He began to ponder how he was going to provide her with the life she deserved. He had promised her the best life when they got married. A house in the suburbs, with a swimming pool, an electric stove and a brand-new Singer sewing machine. He would build a bar in Arcadia where there was a wider clientele for his business. He would hire someone to work with him at the bar who would close up whilst he went home early to help Natsai put buttons on her orders and to spend time with his family. It broke his heart that he was not able to fully provide for his family and give them what they deserved. He thought of his children Nyasha, Rudo and Tendayi. They did not deserve to be treated differently because of their mother and because of him. He understood other things were beyond his control, but he was determined to provide the best for his family regardless.

"Ba T, are you staring at me?" Natsai's words were muffled, her mouth covered by the pillow and her eyes were still closed. It was a rhetorical question, but she enjoyed the different reasons he gave for staring at her. This time, he did not reply. He sighed heavily and put his hand on her back. "Is everything alright?" she questioned him, opening her eyes to look at her husband's face.

"I have been thinking," he confessed. He looked at their asbestos roof which had a hole that he had covered by glueing a piece of wood over it.

"Well, that is a bad idea. You, thinking?" Natsai tried to joke with her husband, but he did not laugh. She noticed how his face grew even more serious. He did not tickle her like he always did when she said something witty.

"Natsai, are you happy? Honestly, are you happy with this?" he said, gesturing his hand around the room to show what he meant. He sighed deeply once more and became silent, again thinking of how he was going to get them out of their predicament. He had been content living in Mufakose all this while, amongst people who had different opinions on why he was amongst them. He was fully aware of it, but he could not leave his family. He could take the misunderstandings. But ever since Allan had come to visit a few nights before, he had been having a change of heart.

"Are you truly happy?" he asked her again, turning to face her. "You can tell me the truth."

"I am comfortable. We have talked about this. We cannot change the leaders of this country, but we can enjoy what we can whilst we still have the chance." Natsai now sat up on the bed, fastening her bonnet.

"Mai T, remember what I promised you when we got married? I feel like I have failed you as a husband and as a man. None of what I promised you has come to pass. I promised to make sure your sewing business would be successful and you would get a contract under my name from Power Sales or even Woolworths. I have failed you." He scoffed with tears in his eyes. Natsai knew and understood what he meant. She had tried to divert the topic each time Tom said something along those lines. She knew it would force her to talk about her hopes and dreams of being a teacher that were thwarted because of love. How she wished they could escape and just be a family without worrying about what people thought of their union. Friends and family had abandoned her for her decision and she had been bitter about it. It hurt her to have to think of how her children would never have grandparents nor ever be fully accepted, how her neighbours called her a traitor for marrying the enemy. He would never be ready for such a conversation. She had made her peace knowing she would never be fully or truly happy, but she was comfortable and that was good enough.

"Ba T please, it is still early in the morning. Are we not a family? Do we not have a roof over our head and do we not have healthy children who are loved? What else can I ask for?" She got up from the bed, a little frustrated.

"Mai T, you and the children deserve better. I want you to be happy, to experience happiness. To have that new Singer sewing machine you have dreamt of. For the children to go to a good school where they do not have to share a book with ten other people. I cannot do this anymore. *We* cannot die like this. *Kwete*," he vowed as he stood up and walked towards his wife who was now gathering her toiletries to prepare for a wash before waking the kids for school.

"So, what are you thinking? Do you have a plan, or you are just dreaming out loud this early? Huh? Tell me, what is your plan for us to escape *this*?" she gestured with her hand as he had before. She did not want to face him with her eyes that were burning with tears. She had abandoned all hope of ever leaving Mufakose and she had wrapped herself in that bubble. She had stopped herself from dreaming or thinking otherwise. Tom's "hope" was slowly dismantling her wall, but unlike Tom, she did not have the luxury to hope.

"I do not have one." he replied, feeling defeated but determined. He tried to hold her, but he knew his answer had thwarted any ounce of optimism in her. He heard her sneer at his response and he knew he had hit a nerve. He knew his wife believed in actions more than words.

"Then let us not talk about it. What is the point of us having hope when there is no way forward?" She turned around and looked at him, her eyebrows furrowed and a tuft of her hair escaping from her bonnet. Tom walked towards his wife and stopped when she reached for her *zambia* which she quickly wrapped around her waist. She left the room without saying anything.

***

Over the past four days, Tunga and Vongai had got the hang of their routine to keep the baby safe and a secret. Vongai would wake up around 4 am as usual, prepare the milk and put out clean baby clothes which she had managed to buy from Natsai. She had told her they were for her sister Mazvita, who had just had a baby. Natsai had not wanted to ask too many questions because the two of them were not particularly close friends, even though Mazvita was about the same age as Nyasha, Natsai's first born who was ten years old.

Vongai would get ready for work and alert Tunga when she was leaving. Tunga, who started work at 8 am and only had to walk thirty minutes to get to work, would wake up around 6:30 am, the same time the baby usually woke up. He would wash him, change him and give him his bottle whilst he got ready for work. They had noticed that he immediately fell asleep after being fed and burped. Tunga would rock him, staying on the lookout for Chenjerai and Gumi who came to get him on their way to work. He would stand by the window in clear view of the *sendiraini* from which Chenjerai and Gumi would emerge with their picks and shovels. When he saw them arrive, he would place the baby in the basket, leaving it open with a mosquito net on top. Tunga made sure he was safe and nothing would trouble his breathing. He then prepared a bottle for when Vongai came home after faking sickness, as they had planned the night before. He also left a glove with soaked rice on the baby's stomach. One that was not too heavy but was light enough to make it feel like a hand on the baby's stomach. It was an idea Vongai had come up with to have the baby believe he was not alone. Tunga had thought it ridiculous at first, but it seemed to work. He made sure to close all the windows except for the one in their bedroom which he opened slightly to let in fresh air. He would finally go to the back of the house where the bedroom was and survey the premises before leaving.

"*Ko mudhara,* can I spend a penny? I left the house in a hurry because of Gumi." It was Chenjerai who asked as he walked past Tunga, making a beeline for the back of the house where the toilet was, outside. Gumi shook his head as he looked on, drawing on the stab of cigarette he had in his hand.

"Ah *shaa,* we are late. You can hold it in," Tunga responded, holding Chenjerai's arm. Chenjerai shrugged him off and continued to walk towards the back of the house.

"Chenjerai! *Shaa ndati* we are late! We do not have time." Tunga grabbed Chenjerai by the arm again and pulled him towards the road.

"Aah *mudhara,* how far? I will not b..." Chenjerai tried to explain but Tunga was not interested. Gumi began to walk towards the road. He had no interest in being the voice of reason, so he made a run for it before they could consult him.

"Let's go, you can go behind the big Msasa tree on our way," Tunga suggested, walking behind Chenjerai who seemed annoyed. "Ah but *mudhara* Tunga, you do not have to treat me like a child," Chenjerai snapped. "I see you won't have any trouble raising kids. You are already equipped *ka.* Too strict over nons..." Chenjerai muttered, but the rest of his sentence was inaudible as he brisked up his pace to catch up with Gumi. Tunga was not paying attention to his friend. Instead, he was listening attentively to any sound coming from the house. After he was certain that there was no crying or whimpering, he ran after his friends, certain Vongai would make it back before he woke up.

***

An hour later, Vongai ran towards her house when she saw Mai Dudzai standing by her door. She appeared to be peeping through the corner of the window to see if there was anyone inside.

"Mai Dudzai, *kwakanaka*? Is everything alright?" Vongai exclaimed, trying to catch her breath at the same time.

"Ah, Mai Kufa I came to check if anyone was in the house because Nhamo and Zivanai came running in the house saying they heard a strange noise in your house when they were playing behind there," Mai Dudzai explained, pointing at the back of Vongai's house and standing behind Vongai who was fumbling with her keys, trying to get in. She had made it a point to always call Vongai by her husband's name, even though Vongai had insisted she called her by her own name.

"Ah, maybe it is one of those stray cats that got in again. I will have to tell Ba Kufa to do something." Vongai unlocked the door and turned to face Mai Dudzai who was eagerly standing behind her.

"Hmm, I do not think so. At first, I thought they were being children and I even beat Nhamo because he kept opening the door and letting the dust into the house. Can you imagine?" Mai Dudzai was trying to peep through the door as Vongai walked into the house.

"Hmm, thank you. I will see to it from here," she responded, trying to close the door behind her, but Mai Dudzai held it and tried to get in

"Ah, Mai Kufa, what if it is something more serious? Let me i..." Mai Dudzai said.

"No! I am fine. Tunga will be here soon, so...so there is nothing to worry about." Vongai slammed the door and locked it as soon as she closed it.

"Very strange of her! Is she hiding something?" Mai Dudzai said to herself as she stood by the door, fixing her *zambia*. She considered going to the back of the house to investigate for herself. She had always thought Vongai was too private and never interacted with the other neighbours. Mai Tafura her other neighbour, had suggested it was because she was a nurse and she had a husband who came back home even on payday and this made her feel superior. Mai Dudzai tiptoed to the back of the house and walked towards the toilet. She saw the light from the bedroom window and just as she was about to walk over to listen and peek through the window, Nhamo came calling for her.

"*Amai,* Zivanai burnt the beans for tonight's supper. The fire is out and all the beans are on the floor," Nhamo reported, standing a distance from her mother.

"Aah, these children. Do you know how hard it was to get those beans? You think it is easy?" she hissed, walking towards Nhamo who was now walking fast towards their house knowing what was to follow.

Vongai heard Mai Dudzai pacing towards her house as she held the baby in her arms. He was fast asleep, but she saw streaks of tears on his face, evidence that he was the cause of the noise that had been reported by the neighbours. She changed him and tried to wake him up with a bottle, but he was in a deep sleep. Vongai put him on the bed and covered him before going into the kitchen to prepare dinner. Tunga had boiled some meat and cut the vegetables when he had come back during his last break.

She knew their routine would not be permanent, but she had not expected it to be disrupted this soon. She and Tunga had not yet come to a concrete plan, only suggestions. She had proposed taking the baby to the hospital and leaving him outside the children's ward without anyone seeing her. She had been examining every passage and entrance on her breaks and after work. Tunga had not been fully committed to her plan. He did not want her to get in trouble or for the baby to be taken away from them and be given to someone who did not care.

"No, you cannot leave *our*… the baby in the bush for three hours Vongai, *pafunge*. What if someone takes him?" Tunga had said the last time they had the conversation.

"Ah, *saka toita sei*? I could wake up earlier and drop him off at 3 am so no one sees me," she suggested, even though that was the conclusion she had come to.

"No! You know around three he will be awake and that is the time when he is most active. You should see him trying to talk." Tunga chuckled and rocked the baby who was babbling away in his arms.

"*Saka todini*? What should we do? Because we cannot keep up with this routine? We need to come up wi– " Tunga cut her off mid-sentence.

"Vongai, relax. We will find a solution. Isn't that right child?" he said, now talking to the baby who was cooing in his arms. "Listen to your mother getting worried. Tell her we will be alright in Smith's Rhodesia." He began to laugh, looking at Vongai.

Vongai saw that her husband was not going to help her come to a solution. He had become too attached to the baby and had forgotten keeping the baby was never a permanent solution. He now came home straight after work and rarely spent time with his friends. Chenjerai had complained the last time she saw him, saying Tunga and Fungai were now forcing him to marry regardless of the UDI's rules and regulations that had stripped black people of imagining a happy life. She saw that she was the one who had to come up with a solution. She was certain Mai Dudzai would pay a visit to investigate and quench her thirst for gossip.

Vongai shook her head. From where she stood by the Primus stove, she peeped into the bedroom where the baby was sleeping. The smoke began to get into her eyes, the smell of paraffin choking her, forcing her to open the window. Her mind reverted to the predicament at hand. She quickly turned off the Primus stove, took the baby, placed him in the basket and left the house.

Vongai arrived at Sangano shebeen as Natsai was getting ready to open for the evening. She was at the back, arranging crates and taking cartons of *Chibuku* out of the old cupboard which hoarded all the stock. Natsai was startled when she saw Vongai standing by the back door. She did not say anything although the look on her face spoke volumes.

"Oh goodness *Vongai*, you startled me. Are you well?" Natsai asked.

"Ye…no. I mea…I need your help," Vongai stammered, looking at the basket in her hand.

"Oh, alright. Please come in. *Pindai,* so we can properly talk." Natsai gestured for her to get into the shebeen. Natsai was a bit perplexed. She was not close enough with Vongai to even consider her a friend. She always thought of her as a sister in arms, waking up every morning to face the world with a smile regardless of how it spat in her face. She was confident the request would not be something out of the ordinary. Maybe she wanted to exchange the baby clothes she had bought a week ago or maybe she wanted a bottle of whiskey for herself. Howbeit, she was not prepared for what Vongai asked and revealed as they sat inside the shebeen.

"Are you out of your mind! Why would you bring this here? And why me?" Natsai jumped out of her seat when she saw the baby in the basket, his blue and bright eyes fully open, sucking on his fists. She could not believe her eyes. Vongai just sat there, looking at her but not saying anything.

"Vongai, please. Get out, please. Leave my house. You want us to get killed?" Natsai continued as she stood with her hands on her waist.

"No, y…you are the only person I could think of. Please help me. I need help to protect him," Vongai explained, holding the baby.

"I am sorry, but I do not see how this is my problem. Please leave!" Natsai shouted, starting to panic. She knew the capital punishment of doing things that were against the law. She had given her life up for one white man, but she was not willing to lose her life for another. She could not believe this was happening to her. She had been content admiring Vongai from afar.

Vongai explained her predicament to the now irritable Natsai. She gave her all the details of how she had ended up taking the baby and how they had been keeping it without anyone knowing for the past three weeks. She confided in her how she did not want a baby for herself but abandoning this one was not an option. She told her about the routine she and Tunga had grown accustomed to, how they knew it would only be temporary although they had not thought it would be so soon they had to find a different solution.

"I know we are not the best of friends and I do not know why I ended up coming here. I jus... please," Vongai concluded.

Natsai paced in the shebeen, trying to think rationally. If she were to accept and keep the baby, how would she take care of it? How would she explain it to her inquisitive children and what would she tell Tom? She knew she had to do something before her customers started coming in for the evening. She sat beside Vongai who was now more relaxed than before. She looked at the baby and could not imagine how anyone would abandon such a helpless child. She decided to stall, to tell Vongai that she had to discuss with Tom first before she could come to any decision. This was her way of politely saying no.

"I wish I could help you more quickly but let me discuss it with my husband first before we do anything."

"Oh, will he be back soon b– "

"Ah, please go. We will see to it tomorrow. He has gone to Arcadia for stock," Natsai said, already getting uncomfortable with her lie. "I need to open up now."

Vongai quietly stood up and headed towards the door with Natsai behind her, escorting her out. They had just got to the door when Tom opened it, holding Rudo in his arms. She was holding *chikendikeke*, giggling, as her father tickled her. The two women stood in silence, looking at the two guests who had joined them. Natsai greeted her husband before sending her daughter to go and tell her sisters it was time to do their homework. Rudo kissed her father and hurried out of the door, her snack in her hand, trotting to find her sisters.

***

Natsai gawked at her husband and took extra blankets from the top of their wardrobe. She could not believe he had agreed to keep the baby whilst Vongai and Tungamirai looked for a more convenient plan. She had listened to Vongai narrate her story to her husband, as emotional as she was before. Natsai was empathetic with her, but she did not feel she had to help. She already had her own predicaments and adding another one was not going to help or make it any easier, even if it was the kind thing to do.

"Natsai, it is only for a while. A few days and things will be back to normal," Tom said, trying to pacify his wife, but Natsai threw the blankets on the floor.

"Tom, where will we keep the baby? Huh, we hardly fit in this house as it is. How is this going to help us get a better life?"

"I am doing this for us. For us to have a better life, Natsai."

"How? Please, tell me. How is this making things better?" She looked at her husband. "I know you have a good heart, and that is one of the reasons I fell for you, but you have to reason too. What are we going to tell people when they hear a baby crying or when the girls start saying things to their friends? You know Nyasha, your daughter cannot keep her mouth shut." she said as she sat on the bed.

"April fourth," Tom said. It was a thing they did when they got into a disagreement or argument which could not be resolved at that time. They would take time to cool off and think. Natsai stood up and walked to the door.

"I am going to put the girls to bed." She walked out without waiting for Tom's reply. Tom watched his wife leave and sighed. He looked at the baby who was sleeping in his arms. He could easily pass as his child. The baby had his blonde hair, his blue eyes and white skin, although Tom's had darkened due to over thirty years under the African sun. He put the baby on the bed and he began to cry. He picked him up and memories of his three daughters doing the same a couple of years ago flooded him.

"You are a blessing in disguise, aren't you? Hee?" he whispered to the baby. "God, is this a sign? Is this what you deem right?" he said, looking up first, then at the baby who was fast asleep again.

***

"Shuvai, think about it. I love you and you love me. What else are we waiting for? Let us just get married." Gumi spoke matter-of-factly. They had been courting for over nine months now. Gumi had been trying to marry Shuvai since the day he met her. She was someone no one would ever think to bring to their mother, but something about her drew her to him: her rebellion against the characteristics of an ideal woman. She was gentle, kind and poised, but many quickly judged her smoking, drinking and fashion sense which they considered unacceptable. She worked as a secretary at the Rhodesia bus company, where black people were allowed.

"Gumi," She sighed heavily, blowing the smoke in the opposite direction from him, "I already told you where I stand with this marriage thing. You and I, we enjoy each other as it is. Why bring marriage into this? We are two people who clearly love each other, I do not see what a piece of paper has to prove," she explained, stroking his face with her free hand. Gumi decided to leave the subject, but he resolved to revisit it later.

They were having a picnic at the Hunyani River just outside of Salisbury. It was their tradition to go there once a month to enjoy themselves with friends. This time, they had brought Vongai and Tunga who sat at a distance from them, gazing at the children who were playing near the river, practising their diving and swimming in the murky water. The pair had their basket in front of them and appeared to be having a serious conversation.

"My eye has been twitching for a couple of days now. I hate it when it does that. Do you think something bad will happen?" Vongai rubbed her eye.

"Hmm, you and your superstitions. Blood is meant to circulate. I know you think it means something bad is going to happen, but no." Tunga responded, turning to look at his wife.

"Tunga, you know how seriously I take these things. Remember the last time it happened, mother fell and broke her hip and now she cannot walk properly. It always means something bad is going to happen."

"So, what bad thing is going to happen now?" Tunga chuckled as he lit a cigarette.

"I know you are making fun of me. You laugh but I can feel it."

Vongai watched her husband as he continued to laugh. It was the first time she had seen him laugh in over a month since she took the baby to Tom's house. He had been enraged when he came back home and found out what she had done. She had explained to him what had happened with Mai Dudzai, but he would not hear of it. She had known he was attached to the baby, but not so much that he would not talk to her for three weeks. He had stopped sleeping in the bedroom and slept on the sofa in the lounge-diner. He came back home late and when Vongai went to work, he slept on the sofa. Tom had agreed with Vongai that they would come and visit at certain times when they wouldn't alert their prying neighbours, but Tunga could not bring himself to do that. He felt something had been stolen from him. He felt his sense of masculinity had been stripped, not only by Vongai for not involving him in her decision, but by now having to be told when to see *his* son. He felt reduced as a black person, as someone who was not able to make it without the help of a white saviour.

Tunga had stopped going to Sangano shebeen because he was unable to face Tom. He felt ridiculous loathing someone who was helping him, but he was jealous and angry at how Tom could have anything he wanted without question because of who he was. He was angry too at how he had been betrayed and he missed the baby. The only person he could confide in was the one he could not turn to. He did not know what to say to her. He felt he had failed her as a husband by not coming up with a solution sooner. He had failed to protect his family, and his wife, out of fear, had acted on his behalf to try and save them.

He looked at Gumi and Shuvai who were sharing an apple and laughing. He turned to his wife who was flicking gnats off her arm. They had been circling over them for a while now and Vongai was becoming annoyed. At that moment Tunga could not deny how beautiful and precious his wife was. He helped her flick some gnats off and drew on his cigarette.

"Last night, before you came back home, Chenjerai came to see me." Tunga paused to blow out the smoke. "He said he felt he had to see me before he left for Chivhu to see his grandmother. He was going on and on about how as men we had to stick together and fight for freedom. He was drunk and he went on and on about how he has appreciated me and loved me as his big brother."

"And what did you say to him?" Vongai asked, rubbing her eye.

"Nothing. I just poured him the last of the brandy and we toasted to a full and free life to come. It is what we can hope for, isn't it?" Tunga looked across the river where the children were becoming fewer as the sun went lower.

"Yes, I guess," Vongai responded.

"I think it's time to go. Gumi and Shuvai are packing their basket. *Handei.*" Tunga stood up and stretched before helping his wife up. The four of them decided to walk home, even though it was quite some distance and they talked and laughed all the way. They bid each other farewell and each couple made their way to their respective humble abodes.

As they turned the corner into their road, Vongai saw a little girl sitting by her door. She could not make out who it was, but she seemed familiar. She was knocking on their door and looking through the front window to see if anyone was home. Tunga and Vongai walked quickly towards the house.

"Hello, how can I help?" Vongai asked as they approached the house. When the girl heard the voice, she turned around and saw the couple holding a basket. It was

Rudo, Tom and Natsai's last born. She was breathing heavily and her knees, legs and hair were dusty and ashy, evidence that she had been playing in the streets.

"Good afternoon? *Baba* said you should come to the house now," she reported, seeming distracted by the children across the road playing *maflawu*.

"Is something wrong? Is *he* alright? Is it the baby?" Vongai was already panicking. She handed the basket to Tunga who was unlocking the door.

"I do not know, they just sent me to call you both and tell you to hurry." Rudo was already running towards the children playing on the road. Vongai realised she was oblivious to why they had been called. She and Tunga left Rudo to join the children who were playing across the street and rushed towards the shebeen.

On arrival, the shebeen was empty and dark, an unusual thing on a Saturday night. They met a couple of gentlemen grunting in annoyance at the shebeen being closed. They went to the back and knocked softly. Tom opened the door and let them in. He looked nervous and he was sweating profusely. Tunga followed his wife in, walking closely behind her as Tom closed the door.

"What happened? Where is he? Is he alright?" Tunga asked without greeting Tom who was still standing by the door.

"Y…Yes, he is alright. It is j…I am very s…" Tom faltered, still standing by the door. He sighed heavily. Tunga and Vongai looked at each other, confused, not knowing what to make of his response.

"Please come in." Tom said, leading them towards the shebeen which was still dark. He seemed very unsettled.

"Where is Natsai?" Vongai asked, confused. She wanted to know what was going on because Tom's actions were making her nervous.

"She will be back soon. She has gone to the market."

As Tunga and Vongai got further into the shebeen, Tom turned on the light. Before them stood four policemen with sjamboks and a German Shepard sitting in the corner. It did not take long for Vongai and Tunga to realise what was taking place. Tunga pulled Vongai and held her tightly.

"So, you are the kaffirs who have been living freely without facing the consequences of your sins?" a familiar voice bellowed. It sent chills down Vongai's spine. When she recognised the voice and saw the face of its owner, she was paralysed. Her knees almost buckled underneath her, but she held on to Tunga who stood quietly. She knew even if he was as terrified as she was, he would never show it.

"Answer me!" the owner of the voice barked again, now walking towards them. "You kaffirs walk around thinking you own this place. You think you could steal a white baby and not face any consequences!" Sergeant Burke lit a cigarette, standing right in front of Tunga. Tunga could feel the warmth of this breath and the pungent smell of cheap whiskey and a foul tongue. He remained quiet. Vongai, on the other hand, began to cry. *How could she be accused of having stolen the baby when she had actually saved it? How were they in the wrong when they had done the right and humane thing to do?* The sergeant moved closer to Vongai and looked at her. He stared at her for a while then drew on his cigarette.

"You look very familiar? Tell me your name?" he asked her, but she did not respond.

"Allan, please. You said you were just going to make them pay you then you would let them go. Tunga, just give him fifty pounds and he will go. Ok?" Tom was still standing by the door. He had done what he had to do. This was his ticket out of Mufakose; a chance to give his family a better life and to fulfil the promises he had made to Natsai.

Sergeant Burke started laughing. The three men behind him all stood at attention, not engaging but ready for any command that might come out of their superior's mouth. "Tom, you are family, but you are very naïve. Let them go? They committed a crime of the highest order. These animals stole a child and brought it to this vapid, disgusting dump of a place? I am taking them in, they will be an example to their kind that the UDI is not to mess with. Nothing goes past us." he paced around the room, pondering what would be the best punishment. He had thought of lashing them in front of the shebeen for everyone to watch, but that had become too common. He yearned to do something that would leave a dent in Mufakose, that would remind everyone that he was the man to be respected and feared.

"Take th… But you promised. You said if I found anything suspicious or out of the ordinary, I should let you know and you would fine them. You never said anything about taking them. Please they are my frie–" Before Tom could finish talking, Tunga punched him in the face. Two of the policemen ran and pinned him down and the other one held Vongai against the wall. Tom started to bleed from his mouth.

"Tunga, I am sorry. I had to look out for my family. This was the only way." The dog started barking, alarmed by the commotion. Vongai was crying, pleading with the policemen to let Tunga go. She confessed she was the one who had taken the baby, but no one gave her their ear. Tunga was on the ground, struggling with the officers.

"How could you? Were you not the one preaching about not being like the rest of them? you son of a bitch, how da–" One of the officers hit Tunga on his back with a sjambok before he could finish talking. He pressed his head down with his arm on his neck and the other one held his legs.

"You see, these people are animals. It is in them, attacking you for doing the right thing. *Sies* man!" Sergeant Burke spat on Tunga and walked towards Tom. "Do not worry brother." He put his arm around Tom. "I knew when I came those few weeks ago, you would help me bring order in this place. I was drunk but I remember every word I said. I just don't remember how I got home hehehe. You know, early that morning I woke up in the bushes, you know by that big Msasa tree?" Tom was paying no mind to him. "Oh brighten up, Tom. You can now leave this dump and start a new life, a new fami…" Tom interrupted him before he could finish.

"What the hell are you on about? Another family for what? You said I would bring my family out. What is this, Allan?" Tom snapped. He was trying to understand what his brother-in-law was saying. Was he implying Tom should leave his wife and children and go by himself? That was not what they had agreed on.

"Oh, do not be daft Tom. You and I both know that is not possible. I only agreed to help *you* leave. I have found a place for you in Mabelreign. It has a pool too. You just leave *all* this behind and start afresh. I promise you will not miss it. And guess what? Hillary is still available." Sergeant Burke casually said this to Tom whose mind was trying to process all that was being said. The dog had settled down now, sitting and waiting for a command.

"Allan! This is not wh… I cannot leave my wife and children. I did *this* for them! How c…" Tom was perplexed. He could not believe he had not seen this coming. Mabelreign was a white only residential area. There was no way on earth he was going to go with his family. He had sacrificed two families because of his selfishness. He knew Natsai would never forgive him, even if he stayed, he had ruined other people's lives. He stood against the wall and slumped on the floor. He put his head in his hands, the damage he had caused dawning on him. He had only been trying to save his family but instead, had ended up breaking it up. He thought of Tunga and Vongai's benevolence, taking that baby in as if it were their own.

Tunga and Vongai were still pinned down. Vongai was fighting the officer who now had a few bruises from being punched and scratched. Tunga was breathing heavily but not making any movement.

"Let us take them in," Sergeant Burke said, lighting up another cigarette. "Tom, I will come around later with the paperwork for your house. The UDI thanks you for your service to your country." He pat Tom on the shoulder and headed for the door. Vongai, who was now in handcuffs, was dragged away by the officer who had been holding her. She kicked and spat on Tom on her way out, but he did not flinch.

"Sir!" the officer who was holding Tunga's head down shouted. "He is not getting up!"

"*Futsek mhani*, get up! Let me speak in a language he understands. *Simuka*." the other officer barked, kicking Tunga in the stomach. Tunga did not move.

They could hear Vongai still crying outside as the officer tried to put her in the back of the Landrover Defender. Tom looked on, paralysed by the thought of what was happening. He could not muster the courage to stand up. He put his head between his knees and remained that way.

Sergeant Burke tramped back into the room. "Get him up, I said!" he bellowed impatiently.

"He is dead, sir.

Farisai

Today I saw Tinashe Chari, the boy I lost my virginity to. There were six people between us in the queue. He stood staring straight ahead, barely moving with a Pick n Pay white plastic bag in his hand. I stood there, staring at his back, hoping he would not turn around because I would be in clear view of him. I could have gone to another bank, but after two hours of standing under the African summer sun in October, leaving the queue was not an option. Street vendors were up and early, with baskets of fruits on top of their heads. Econet, Netone and Telecel juice cards were being shoved in every queuer's face, as we impatiently waited for our turn at the cash machine. A beggar was sitting at the bank entrance, holding an enamel plate, begging for money from those who had woken up at four am to make it in time before the USD cash ran out. I stood, thinking of a way I could maintain my position, standing out of sight just in case something prompted him to turn. He looked taller than I remembered; his shoulders were broader and the white shirt he wore outlined his frame, but even from behind, you could tell he had not grown into his ears.

I could not help but notice his ring finger was naked and he rubbed it with his thumb every now and again. My mind raced back to the time when we were dating in high school, but I could not remember why we broke things off. All I remembered was, I also lost my best friend, Rufaro, on the same day.

The woman behind me had her baby cinched to her back. She called out for one of the vendors who were roaming, trying to guilt us into buying something. She chose a ripe banana and gave it to the toddler who began to eat it the moment her mother handed it to her. The woman ruffled through her handbag looking for the money to pay for the banana.

"*Iiih, mukoma*, I am so sorry, but I am one rand short. Is it ok if you sell them to me for four rands?" she asked, still rummaging in her handbag. The young man who had sold her the banana looked at her, astonished. He shook his head and laughed sarcastically.

"*Ambuya,* you can see we are all looking for money. I woke up early, just like you, to work. In this economy, we cannot afford discounts or *bacossi*. Please, may I have my rand so I can go about my business or else your child might have to vomit that banana," he said, standing next to me, hugging the basket with commodities under his arm. I quietly prayed they would not cause a scene which would draw Tinashe's attention. The lady quietly removed her baby who had already eaten the banana halfway from her back. She took the remainder of the banana and handed it over to the vendor who was still standing there, waiting for his money or the banana.

"Ooh, *tora*. Take it. There is your banana. I do not have enough money and I do not want any problems," she said, handing over the half-eaten banana. The toddler in her arm was confused and reached for her half-eaten meal, but the mother kept moving it away from her whenever she tried to grab it. The vendor put his basket down and scratched his head, looking at the woman with a grin on his face.

"*Imi amai imi!* Madam, are you for real? You are seriously giving me a half-eaten banana? What will I do with it? I want my money, please. *Nyarai shuwa!* Have you no shame? Give me my money!" He shouted, putting his basket down and moving closer to the woman.

"Take the banana. I do not have enough money. You said the money or my baby would have to vomit the banana. Well, here, take the remaining piece. It's better than vomit," she said, trying to put her child on her back. The baby kept reaching for the banana.

"*Iwe, dzikama.* Do you have the money to pay for the banana? Keep quiet!" the mother aggressively snapped at her child who seemed to have understood but ignored her.

They began to argue very loudly, pointing fingers, and the baby began to cry. The queuers began to grumble in their positions, those in the front looking back to see what was happening. I kept my eyes on Tinashe's back. He was talking to the man in front of him.

"*Manje* I am going to stand in line with you until you give me my money. I will not leave, I swear on my ancestors! You have not seen anything yet, this is my business," the vendor said, standing in line beside the woman.

Her baby was now screaming on top of her lungs, muddled by a strange man pointing at her, and her mother handing him the banana she was eating. Moreover, she was tired – as tired as the other fifty-six people standing in the queue. The woman managed to strap her baby on her back and stone-faced, looked forward, ignoring the vendor. He went on swearing on his ancestors, pacing up and down along the queue. He began to attract more attention, involving other people in the discourse.

My eyes were shifting from the scene to Tinashe, whose attention was now on the vendor who had now put his basket down. I tried to hide behind the woman, but she kept moving, trying to settle her child with one hand and pointing at the vendor with the other. I peeped coyly at Tinashe and we locked eyes. I quickly averted mine and looked down. His reaction suggested he did not recognise me. He looked at me like I was another stranger to him. I kept my gaze down for a while longer. *How could he not recognise me?*

Three police officers came to deescalate the situation. However, the woman and the vendor kept shouting and the officers ended up taking them away. The heat was getting to me. It was midday and the queue had not moved for the last thirty minutes. I tried to push the thought of Tinashe out of my mind. It was embarrassing enough, him not recognising me; replaying it would add on to the stress I already had. *But how could he not remember me?*

While my mind was struggling to understand his not remembering me and my not forgetting him, I felt someone tap on my shoulder. I thought it was another vendor trying to lure me into buying their goods, but a voice broke and said my name. I turned around and saw him smiling at me. The same smile that used to warm my insides and make my privates pulsate. "Oh wow, Fari *ndiwe* sure?" he beamed, collecting me into his arms. I took in his scent; a mixture of Colour Me green and a hint of sweat; that manly sweat that is not pungent but awakens a part of you that is usually triggered by hands, tongue and lips. He pulled away and looked at me. It took me a while to come back to reality. "It has been a while, how have you been?" He asked. He looked so happy to see me and I felt the same, but I was not sure if it was for the same reason. I had tried contacting him over the years, and by try, I mean looking through his Facebook and maybe visiting his workplace, a few times a week. The first time was two years ago when I saw his *roora* pictures on Facebook. I bumped into them whilst stalking Rufaro. Our friendship had ended after she told Tinashe I was cheating on him. I wanted to know how her life had turned out after betraying our girl code. She always had that air around her, thinking she was more morally inclined and better than others. She had been tagged in one of the pictures. I guess they remained in touch.

In the picture, I saw Tinashe and his wife, smiling at the camera in matching Ndebele traditional wear. She had a white dress that complimented her dark hue. Some would call her beautiful, but beauty is subjective. I went on to his Facebook page and his timeline was flooded with odes and pictures of his wife. I noticed he had not tagged her on the posts. I decided to go through his friends' list but I could not find her. I concluded she was not on Facebook. I scrolled down his timeline from the day he joined Facebook. He had graduated from MSU with an engineering degree and had secured a good job soon after. I was glad to see he had remained faithful to his dream to be an engineer. Apparently, he had met this *Sophia* at University too. I tried to calculate how long it took him to move on after we broke up.

***

We were walking home from school, the way we always did. I remembered the pain in his voice and the tears in my eyes when he asked me about Takunda – I think that's what his name was. He caught me unaware, I had not prepared my defence. All I could say was, "I can explain."

"Explain then. Tell me the truth, are you being unfaithful, Fari?" he said, sounding more hurt than angry. To this day, I hate how I handled the situation. It was my immaturity that made me lose the only person I ever loved – *still* loved. I gaslit him, told him it was not my fault he could not please me, whilst he was on his knees. I made him believe it was his fault I cheated. "If you could have been man enough and taken care of my needs, *maybe* I would have been faithful," I jeered, sizing him up and down. Tinashe looked confused and defeated. I am sure if I had told him automobile starts with the letter O, he would have believed me. He begged and pleaded, even promised we would move on and he would "man up." I sized him up and down again as he spewed how Rufaro had told him everything and he did not want to believe her. "Puuh!" I spat and began to detest him, his desperation sickening me already. "So, you have been cheating on me with my best friend?" I cackled and clapped my hands slowly. "Do I look stupid to you?" I snapped, starting to walk away from him. I did not turn back even though I heard him call my name several times. His desperation drove him to call me "honeybae" his pet name for me, but I did not flinch.

I remembered how he begged to have me back until our last exam. Even Rufaro, with her trifling behind, tried to get involved again. I told her to face her front and never approach me again. She was my most trusted friend, but she chose to break the girl code. Every girl knew girl code was a commandment, but she had decided to be Judas and sell me over. For what? I cut them both out of my life and decided to live my life how I wanted, but if I am being honest, that has been one of my many regrets.

***

"Hi, ah yes, it has been too long. How have you been?" I asked, pretending I did not already know how his life was. Checking his Facebook and that of his friends had become a daily ritual. Even us meeting at the bank, had not been a mistake. I knew he would be here, I have been following him. What I was not expecting was an encounter with him. I watched his lips as he went on and on about the people we went to school with. Fadzai was now a mother of two and a widow. Shammaine was in the diaspora and an influencer. Oscar was now one of the big boys in Harare and had found a "good" job for Tinashe but his Sophia had talked him out of it, because, according to her, that kind of thing was done by people who did not fear God.

The line began to move forward– thank God – because that stopped Tinashe from going on and on about his wife. We both moved forward and maintained our position. There were people trying to cut the queue but this country has conditioned us to be in constant survival mode. The vendor was back and now he was on another customer, shoving his goods in his face.

"It's good to hear. Such a long queue. I hope we get lucky and get some cash." I was not planning on saying anything, but I just wanted to listen to the sound of his voice, even though what he was saying was not what I wanted to hear. I wanted him to say, I love you and miss you. "Yes *sha*, I have been here since early morning. So, what's new *newe*? How is life?" he asked gleefully.

I had not thought about this. He caught me off guard. "Ah, nothing much. I am a researcher for an independent company. You?" *Yes, I being the company and researching about him*. He had become my obsession.

"Well, I am now working at a bank. The irony of it is me standing in the queue." I already knew he was a banker. All this was not news to me. I pieced it together from his Facebook post from two years ago: *Can someone tell what my next move might be? Riddle me this, what do you call a financial scam in Egypt? Pyramid scheme.*

I never understood the riddle until he posted a picture of himself with an RBZ lanyard. He had always been terrible at jokes, but I missed that and wanted it back. I gave little information about myself, enough to keep him engaged but not ask too much. He, on the other hand, went on and on about his endeavours, how life was getting hard in Zimbabwe and him thinking of leaving. He also raved about his *beautiful* wife. He even laughed about us and how we were so young, he had forgotten about our relationship. I was taken back. My plan of reeling him back into my arms relied on a possible mutual feeling. The hooting of the cars, Tinashe's voice and loud hawkers trying to make a sale were drowned out by the thoughts running through my mind. How was I going to turn this in my favour? He nudged me to move because the queue had moved by a few inches. I watched him speak, looking forward and looking at me only for a response. I gathered the confidence to ask him, but as I was about to open my mouth, his phone rang.

"Hey baby, yeah, I am still at the bank and you will not believe this. I ran into an old high school friend of mine." I smiled back when he smiled at me, still on the phone. I pretended not to eavesdrop and I focused my eyes on a vendor who was counting his money. I heard Tinashe on the phone talking about how he was thinking of moving to Malaysia in three months. I also began to plan on how I was going to get my passport and look for accommodation and a job in Malaysia. The vendor looked up from counting his money and our eyes met.

I smiled at him, but he quickly put his stash away and walked away with his basket of produce on top of his head.

Tamuka

My cousin Tamuka sat with his knees folded in front of Mudzimumitatu and spat out the brownish liquid he had been instructed to drink. All the five elders of the village and Musafare, a close friend of Mukoma Zorodzai, congregated in the small, thatched hut with the intention of finding out what had caused the sudden death. The men sat quietly and observed Mudzimumitatu cast his lots in front of Tamuka who now sat stolid with his head down. I was only allowed to the rite to help Sekuru mobilise, as age had begun to shake hands with his eyesight. Mudzimumitatu, the *n`anga*, was known for his witch hunt expertise and reversing curses all over the villages. He was the one to go to if one wanted a husband, if one wanted to get rid of a husband or if one wanted someone else's husband. He is the reason I can narrate what I saw, being the one who was at the helm of restoring my poor eyesight due to my albinism. He began to chant something in a language that was not amongst the six that were common in the village. The men all sat motionless, gawking at him.

He took a swig from the large clay pot he held in his hands, the same clay pot from which he had instructed Tamuka to drink from. Mudzimumitatu began to dance in a ritualistic style, circling Tamuka, whilst his aide, Mhinduro, began to clap his hands, chanting, "*Huyai, svikai, taurai*," repeatedly as he sat with his head between his knees. The elders joined in and began to clap and chant in unison. Mudzimumitatu dipped low and jumped so high, I thought he would go through the thatched roof. He circled around

Tamuka and stroked him with his staff which had tassels and golden-brown fur. He took another swig and spat at Tamuka then stood behind him. Each swig was met with vigorous claps and louder chanting.

I clapped in unison, not out of awareness of what I was witnessing, but out of fear of Sekuru sending me outside to run errands for the women who were in the cooking hut. I made sure I did not make noise or any sudden movements, knowing Sekuru would see it as a sign of disrespect to the spirits and the importance of the event at hand. The traditional healer raised his right hand, beckoning us to stop chanting and clapping. He took a few steps and knelt in front of Tamuka then held his head in his hands.

"*Taura*, before the turmoiled spirit of your brother undertakes its own justice. Confess my son," he said, now in Shona. Sekuru slowly nodded; in as much as he was as blind as a bat, his hearing was still very sharp. Tamuka said nothing, his eyes fixated on Mudzimumitatu, brimming with tears. He no longer looked like the tall and strong fourteen-year-old who taught me how to make herbal sunscreen for my dry, patched skin. We would race each other the long distance to the Growth Point to buy a small Vaseline and on our way back, picking the rest of the various ingredients in the small forest near the compound. As he sat in front of us, he looked shrunken and helpless.

"Are you sure you have nothing else to confess aside from what you have told the congregation?" Mudzimumitatu continued, still holding Tamuka's head. Tamuka uttered a yes and tried to look down again, but Mudzimumitatu would not let him. He began to make a roaring sound, a poor imitation at first, but after a while sounded as real as that of the king of the jungle. It was said to be one of the three spirits that possessed him: *shumba* introduced himself with a roar and the host's body displayed a menacing facial expression, his body rigidly standing at attention, feet apart, arms hanging and his palms in fist formation. The *shumba* spirit was known for being stern and interrogatory, leaving its prey on its hands and knees begging for mercy.

Legend has it, if angered or deceived, the *shumba* spirit asks the *sabhuku* to have all the elders in the village bring beer made from finger millet to the *sabhuku*'s *hozi.* Each morning, for three consecutive days, Mudzimumitatu sits at the door of the accused before sunrise and laments to the spirit of the dead to reveal themselves in the house of the accused. A few moons ago, in Hwedza, the village east of ours, a woman who was accused of permanently disposing of her newborn children was asked to confess why all her children died within three weeks of being born. Rumour has it, it was because she wanted constant attention and sympathy from people since her husband worked in Harare and would only come home four times a year. She would always claim she was cursed or unlucky because even after being prayed for by prophets and pastors and being to the traditional healers, all her six children died, either at birth or a few weeks after. For the ones that died at birth, I once heard Mai Kwayedza, the village midwife, tell Sekuru that during birth she closed her legs when the head was out. On the third day in this particular case, Mudzimumitatu had the village crier summon the whole village to the cemetery where they found the woman with five small skeletons carefully placed next to her as if they were asleep, holding a small rotting corpse, which she was trying to nurse.

The *shumba* spirit huffed and puffed around Tamuka. He asked him to stand and face the west and call Mukoma Zorodzai's name. Tamuka did as instructed. He was told to narrate his story again as he faced the wall. Mhinduro began to take out different objects from Mudzimumitatu's *nhava.* Some of the objects looked very strange. There was an object that looked like Sekuru's *nhekwe,* but it was big and was wrapped with snakeskin. He unwrapped it and placed a carving of a snake, positioning it behind Tamuka. My cousin began to narrate the story of how Mukoma Zorodzai was found dead in the bottle store after Tamuka had taken his *mbuva* for that day to him.

It was last week Friday when Maiguru gave Tamuka Mukoma Zorodzai's *mbuva* to take to him at the growth point where he spent most of the afternoon playing *njuga.* It was Mukoma Zorodzai's birthday, and to celebrate, Maiguru had killed for him the last hen on the compound. I remember Tamuka telling me he had been annoyed by this because he had planned to take Sekuru's cockerel and have it mate with the hen. He recounted how Maiguru instructed him to take it straight to him and not pass through our compound as he always did. She had warned him to deliver the food whilst it was still hot or else Mukoma Zorodzai would be in one of his moods when he came back. He recalled how Maiguru had a black eye and busted lip, evidence of the row they had had the previous night as on every other night. He had told me he had heard muffled screams and hollow *diii diii* sounds from his *gota.* Tamuka confessed that on his way, he had only taken a few minutes off course into the forest to look for *matohwe* which were in season. He said as he was walking back to the road, he came across a herb that was a perfect remedy for *man'a.* The herb was crushed, mixed with water and just a smidgen of the venom of a *rovambira.* He had learnt all this from his father, whom he shared with Mukoma Zorodzai albeit with different mothers. He said after picking the herb, he stuffed it in his pocket and proceeded to go to the Growth Point. He reported he did not recollect touching the food with his hands, knowing how poisonous the herb was, but remembered shaking hands with Mukoma Zorodzai.

As soon as he confessed this, sneers and hollers broke out. Everyone knew Mukoma Zorodzai never washed his hands. That is why at every gathering, he was always given his own plate. People had made him believe it was because he was well respected amongst the men, but it was solely because of his habit of licking his fingers with every bite and never washing his hands before his meals. It was only a matter of time until his quirk caught up with him. The only unfortunate part was Tamuka being inculpated of it.

Tamuka began to cry, facing the wall. I wanted to go over to him and comfort him, but I knew better. Mhinduro raised his right hand, commanding silence in the room. Mudzimumitatu was, at this moment, sitting on the floor with his knees folded and head down. He uttered a strange noise and within a few seconds, he was hissing. I do not want to believe it, but I know what I saw. His skin began to shimmer and took on a darker hue. He began thrusting his tongue in and out of his mouth like a snake. Mhinduro instructed all of us to cover our heads and to shield our eyes. Out of curiosity, which I now regret, I saw him lying on the floor and begin to slither around Tamuka the way a snake does. His aide launched a dead rat which I think he had taken from his *nhava* and threw it towards the traditional healer. Just like a snake, he leapt and caught the rat whilst it was still in mid-air. I saw him swallow it whole and repose on the floor. Mhinduro began the chant and rhythmic clap again and we all joined in. He darted his eyes at me, but I quickly closed mine.

"*Zvakanaka mwanangu.* All is well. I know my children very well and soon you shall see their true colours. I, their mother, have spoken. You shall see them by their fangs, their scaled skin and their deceitful ways," a croaky, female voice spoke. I could not see a woman but when I glanced at Mudzimumitatu, his lips were moving in unison. I involuntarily jounced with fear. My eyes and ears could not fathom what I was witnessing. Sekuru turned towards me, reached for my ear and pulled it so hard I could feel blood well up. He did not say anything to me, but I clearly knew what he meant. I sat up properly and paid attention to the event at hand, slowly rubbing my ear. Mhinduro took out another small container from his *nhava*, this one was covered in crocodile skin, with a string that appeared to have teeth attached to it. He unwrapped it and took out a small carving of a crocodile. He summoned us to start the chant again, louder and with vigour. This time he did not instruct us to look away. Still lying on the floor, Mudzimumitatu stretched his legs and arms away from his body and slightly lifted himself off the floor. He resembled the posture of a crocodile, although his scraggy figure did not do him justice. His *mhapa* and *shashiko* were coming undone in this action-packed ritual. I quickly looked away from his male member that was beginning to show as he began to belly crawl around the room. His eyes were blinking rhythmically and with each blink, the colour of his eyes appeared to change. Tamuka still stood facing the wall. He had stopped crying but I could sense his fear from where I was sitting.

Mudzimumitatu let out a loud hiss which caught Sekuru off guard, almost toppling him over from the stool he sat on. I quickly helped him up and went back to my designated seat. We were ordered to be silent. Mhinduro began to sprinkle the liquid that was in the clay pot on Mudzimumitatu who began to breathe heavily, his aide prancing around him in circles.

"Why do you summon me when the one before me has revealed the truth?" his voice thundered across the room. It was no longer the brittle voice that had alarmed me earlier.

"*Munondinyaudzirei!* I am of the water, return me to the water where I belong." The elders looked at each other and then at Tamuka. He still seemed like himself and there was nothing out of the ordinary. Was it a hoax? Had Mudzimumitatu now lost his touch? They all began to mumble amongst themselves. Had they been cooped up in this small hovel for nothing? Mhinduro began to pack their belongings. Mudzimumitatu sat on the floor, leaning against the wall, perspiring and drinking from one of the clay pots filled with water. He no longer looked as menacing as before, his skinny legs stretched out as he gulped down the water.

"*Pangu ndapedza*, as you have heard the spirit say. If you may guide Mhinduro to your kraal to fetch my cattle, I would very much appreciate it," he suggested, getting up to leave. The elders scratched and shook their heads, at a loss for words, but afraid to say anything out of fear of being cursed.

"*Ah varume,* what is th– " Musafare was cut mid-sentence by a loud wail that came from the direction of the kitchen. All the men scrambled out of the *hozi* to investigate.

"*Mwari wangu,* Mai Pamidzai *kani! Yuwi, heano mashura!*" Mai Kwayedza cried as she ran towards the men. As soon as she reached them, she fainted. Behind her, Kwayedza was not far behind, terror plastered on her face. Musafare ran towards her and held her before she collapsed. He interrogated her as she lay limp in his arms.

"What is it? Speak. *Chii chaitika*?" he asked.

"Mai Pamidzai. She tur–"

"You mean Zorodzai's wife? Is it? What happened? *Iwe taura*." he asked, vigorously shaking her so she would stay conscious.

"*Vawira musadza.* She fell into the pot of sadza," she reported, tears running down her face.

The elders all looked at each other, confused and getting annoyed. These women always made everything dramatic.

Mai Kwayedza was still on the ground, motionless and no one was attending to her.

"What are you saying? *Asi wakupenga?* Are you going mad?" Musafare barked at her. I stood next to Sekuru who listened attentively. Tamuka had now joined us but stood at a distance.

"Mai Pamidzai was cooking sadza a–and as she was mixing the sadza in the big pot. Sh–she just fell in. I think it was her, I do not know." she began to cry, trying to free herself from Musafare's grip.

"*Iwe taura. What do you mean* she fell into the pot? Did you help her out?"

"Y–yes, but instead of her, w–we found a snake."

At that, the elders hurried over to the kitchen. They could hear the clamour of women and children, shouting and crying. I stayed behind with Sekuru who reached over to Tamuka and held him close.

"My job here is done," Mudzimumitatu said as he herded four cattle out of the compound, Mhinduro following not far behind him with his *nhava.*

Pamushana

"Gogo, can a person be in love with two people at the same time?" Chido innocently asked as her grandmother plaited her hair. It was their ritual; every other Saturday after all the chores were done and the raspy voice of Oliver Mtukudzi was blasting from the cassette player her father had won at the OK Grand Challenge, Gogo would call her to come outside *pamushana* and plait her hair. She always had a new hairstyle which she picked from the *Parade* magazine. Chido enjoyed these moments, the warmth of her grandmother's thigh against her ear when she plaited the sides, the way her fingers massaged her scalp as she applied the hair food and pudding. It was the closest she ever got to human intimacy with her parents being in South Africa and only visiting during public holidays.

She loved having Gogo's undivided attention. It was just the two of them and she knew in those moments, she could ask her anything. At nine years old, Chido still had the innocence of being able to ask any question without being perceived as rude or ill-mannered, evident by the time she asked Mai Takura why she only acknowledged her when her mother came back from South Africa and why she would leave with a plastic bag full of the goodies which her mother had brought. Mai Takura only laughed her off. Her mother gave her a look that narrated how the night was going to end for her. But Gogo always entertained her zeal. That night, after Chido's mother had given her a beating that left her questioning her mother's love, Chido went to the spare room which she shared with Gogo and slept on her side of the bed.

Gogo stretched out her hand and rubbed her back until she fell asleep. Gogo had always been a woman of few words, but she was always observant. She had volunteered to stay with Chido when her son got a job in South Africa and Maidei, Chido's mother, had refused to stay behind and become a *was wife*. Chido could not go with them because for Maidei to go, she had had to get a job which meant no one would have been available to stay at home to take care of Chido. Her parents could not just leave her with anyone because Maidei had heard how house helpers and maids were feeding their bosses' children menstrual blood as vengeance for unfair treatment and wages.

"*Saka uri kuda ndidini*? I cannot go with the both of you and in this economy, you know I need to take this job. You have to stay." Chamai, Chido's father, had tried to explain to his wife two years ago. He spoke as he lit a cigarette, sitting on the edge of their three-quarter bed. The smoke wafted through their broken window, which was covered by a plastic bag. The bag was now tattered after being poked by Chido.

"Over my dead body! You will not leave me here and go to Johannesburg and philander there. You and I are leaving on that Intercape coach next week," Maidei informed her husband. *How dare he think she would end up like the other women who had been left by their spouses.* Mai Takura and Shuvai's relationships had suffered at the hands of South Africa's greener pastures and big-bosomed, light-skinned *ntombazanas*. Because of them, Ba Takura had become a myth and Tapiwa, Shuvai's boyfriend whom she had already raised money with for their wedding, had gone to South Africa to find the best suppliers for their wedding and had not come back. It had been four years.

"*Saka uri kuda kuti ndidini*? What do you want me to do?" Chamai asked his wife again. He knew how she always got caught up in the neighbourhood gossip. She always projected other people's problems and opinions on their family. When Sekai from three houses down had raised her voice at her mother, the rumour had circulated that it was because she had grown too big for her breeches and since then, Maidei had stopped entertaining Chido's many questions and had instructed her to call her *amai*.

"Ah, why are you asking me? Are you not the head of the house? The leader of the house? Lead us to a solution with common sense. *Asi ziva kuti handisi kusara*, I am not staying behind," Maidei had remarked to her husband. Chamai ended up bringing his mother from Njanja, the village in Chivhu where she lived, to stay with their daughter.

"Gogo?" Chido called her grandmother who had remained quiet after she asked the question.

"Why do you ask?" Gogo asked as she parted Chido's hair to make a line.

"Well, at school Tendai told Varaidzo and Rutendo that he loved them both." she shifted a bit from her position. "How is that possible? Are you not supposed to love one person at a time?"

"Hmm, I see," Gogo said and cleared her throat, applying the Blue Magic hair food in Chido's hair. "Do you not love your mother and father at the same time?" she asked her granddaughter. She had sensed her detest for her mother and had seen how she acted when her mother was around. Chido remained quiet. She did not know how to reply. She knew she was supposed to love her mother because she was the one who had given birth to her, but if she was being honest with herself, it was not love she felt for her mother but tolerance.

"Go and fetch me some water and I will tell you a story," Gogo instructed her granddaughter. Gogo stretched herself on the plastic stool she sat on and smiled at the sky with her eyes closed, the sun kissing her face. It was around ten in the morning, just as the sun began to get warmer and inviting. She shifted in her seat and began humming along to *Rudo Runokosha* by Mr Chitungwiza which was now playing on the radio. Tears welled in her eyes. She wiped them away with the back of her hand when she saw Chido emerging from the kitchen with the cup of water. She took it with both hands and gulped the water down while Chido resumed her position.

"*Maita Achinjanja*," Gogo thanked Chido as she placed the cup next to her on the floor. She sang along to the song until it came to an end. She smiled to herself and then began to narrate her story.

"It was in late 1982 and I was about twenty years old when I met him. I had just become a receptionist at Sekenhamo Primary School. He had come for an interview to apply as a Mathematics teacher for the Grade 7 classes. He was very handsome in his white shirt which had pit stains, his brown bell-bottom trousers, black shoes and mini afro. I kept looking at him as he sat in the reception area. He looked nervous but serious. He was holding a plastic file which I presumed concealed his credentials and an afro comb. I had never seen such a handsome man before. All the boys I had grown up around did not possess his regal air. *It must be a Ndebele thing,* I thought to myself." Gogo chuckled as she parted another line. "I kept stealing glances at him, but he did not reciprocate. I offered him water, but he declined politely and thanked me for my generosity. His smile caught me unaware. He had one of those infectious smiles that made you smile back."

"Gogo, was it like when Ngoni smiles showing the gaps in his teeth and it makes me want to laugh?" Chido asked as she giggled, imagining Ngoni's almost toothless smile.

"No, *muzukuru,*" Gogo replied, "It was a nice smile. Beautiful even. And he laughed with his whole body too. He was tall, taller than me, and I was never a short girl. He complimented my height when we took our long evening walks. Ah, look at me getting ahead of myself." She laughed and clapped her hands twice and shook them towards the sky the way she always did when she got excited. "He smiled at me as he went into the office where Mr. Nyedza, the headmaster, was waiting to interview him. I tried to keep myself busy, filing receipts and invoices, updating the school register and typing out the newsletters on the typewriter that had been donated to us. Click-clack, it went as I typed, but I could not focus. I could not wait for him to come out so I could get a good look at him again. After twenty minutes or so, he came out with Mr. Nyedza behind him. They shook hands and wished each other the best of luck. He waved at me as he went out of the door with his file tucked under his armpit. That was the last I saw of him at the school."

"Did you love him Gogo?" Chido asked as she squirmed, trying to make herself comfortable.

"Yes. Yes, I really did," Gogo responded. Seeing that Chido was uncomfortable, she told her to sit up straight so she could plait the middle.

"Did he love you back?" "Oh yes. It was the purest form of love I ever experienced. It was a love that was kind, forgiving, sacrificial and humble. Anyway, where was I?" Gogo asked Chido, not because she was not aware, but to veer her granddaughter back to the story.

"You said you never saw him again Gogo, so how did you love him," Chido asked. "I did see him again, but it was a few months later and it was not at the school. Chiedza and I had gone to a nightclub after work. It was after we were no longer called Rhodesia, so we could roam the city centre unto kingdom come and we were now allowed into places we had never dreamt of going into." She chuckled, remembering how they ran in First Street after Independence Day.

"Who is Chiedza, Gogo?" Chido asked sleepily as she placed her head on Gogo's lap. She always fell asleep when Gogo got to the middle part of her head.

"Chiedza was my friend from ages ago. God bless her soul. She was a wild one that one, but with a big heart; as big as your head," she said, gently nudging at Chido's cheek. Chido let out a soft chuckle and shifted her position.

Gogo remembered how Chiedza and her had drunk Black Label for the first time sitting in one of the restaurants that had only been for white people before Independence. She missed her free and rebellious friend. It saddened her that that same freedom had led to her death in the nineties.

"I was sitting at a table near the bar when he approached me. I was busy searching for Chiedza who had vanished into the crowd with one of her lov–, her friend she had not seen in a while." Gogo made sure she was careful with her words around Chido. "He approached the table and sat next to me. His afro had grown. He was wearing a black viscose shirt with the three top buttons undone and red bell-bottoms. I did not get a chance to see his shoes as the light in the club was dim. But he looked very handsome, yooh, *handsome pfacha chaiyo*."

Chido chuckled at this. She always found the word "*pfacha*" funny. She began to say it repeatedly but quietly so Gogo would not hear her and think she was not listening.

***

"*Wena*, I have seen you before, but I cannot remember where," Dumisani said as he made himself comfortable next to Gogo. His speech was a bit slurred and she could not tell if he was drunk or that was the way he spoke. He flashed a smile at Gogo and she smiled back, a bit nervous but nonetheless eager to talk to him.

"Yes, a few months back you came for an interview at Sekenhamo Primary. I was the recep–"

"Receptionist. Oh, now I remember. I was wondering *vele* where have I seen this beautiful face before," he said, summoning the waiter. Gogo began to blush. *Had he really thought her beautiful or was it just the euphoria of the Dutch courage that inspired him?* He asked if he could buy her a drink and which one she would like. Gogo liked that. He was not like the other men who prowled the club, telling women what they must drink and assuming they would like their drink of choice. The waiter took their order and pushed his way through the crowd of people who were dancing *kongonya* and moonwalking on the dance floor. The atmosphere was sultry, rowdy and musty from the busy bodies celebrating the end of the week.

"*Woza*! I love this song. Come, you have to dance with me," Dumisani said as he walked backwards towards the dance floor, stretching out his hands towards her. He slowly closed his eyes and began to jive, feeling the music and trying to sing along. Gogo realised he did not know the lyrics nor what the song truly meant.

"Come on, dance with me." he said as he carefully pulled her on the dance floor. "I do not fully understand the lyrics, but I know the word *rudo* and that it means love and that is enough for me," he shouted. The clamour had grown louder because of a dance battle beside them. People were cheering for the men who were challenging each other. Dumisani continued dancing. Gogo moved closer and began to follow suit.

"The song is called *Rudo Runokosha* and it is by John Chibadura. We also call him Mr Chitungwiza. He is singing about how love is important in life," Gogo explained as they danced. "Aha! I was right, it has something to do with love." They both laughed and danced, and danced, and danced the night away.

"My name is Dumisani by the way." he said as he walked her home. It occurred to her then that they had danced together all night but had not introduced each other. Gogo introduced herself and thanked him for the eventful night. They tarried for a while, talking about work, family and life. Gogo had altogether forgotten about Chiedza, who, she was sure, was somewhere with one of her lovers.

"There is another vacancy for a Maths teacher at Sekenhamo. You should come and apply again. The one who got the job previously, Mr. Ndlovu, is leaving. He said it was a family issue and he is going to South Africa with his whole family," Gogo said. She had wondered why the man looked paranoid and eager to leave Zimbabwe when they had been given back the country. Zimbabwe was free and it had been three years since their independence, but he preferred to leave for a country that had not gained its independence yet.

"*Haibo*, why would he leave for that Boer country when we are now free? It is time for us sons and daughters of the soil to shine," Dumisani replied, thrusting his fisted arm in the air. Gogo could not keep her eyes off him. His build complimented the strength of his voice. He promised to come to the school the following Monday to apply for the teaching vacancy. They stood for a while, neither of them saying a word.

"Now that I know you are home and safe, I will make my way home." Dumisani broke the silence. Gogo nodded her head in agreement. She shook his hand and held it tightly. He stood staring at her. They could both feel the chemistry. Even though they were both tired, neither of them wanted to leave. The sky was turning orange and the early birds were beginning to welcome a new day. Gogo leaned forward and kissed him. Dumisani pulled her in and kissed her back. They only let go when a car passed them and the driver shouted for them to get out of the road and get a room. "You have no idea how long I have been wanting to do that," Dumisani said bashfully and scratched his head, shying away from Gogo, who was shocked by her act but unapologetic. She gave him a light peek on the cheek and walked to her house. Dumisani smiled as he watched her walk home, certain this was the beginning of something special.

For three weeks Gogo and Dumisani enjoyed each other's company. On their lunch breaks at work, they would sit at the school grounds on the terraces and share a chicken pie and a bottle of Fanta. They introduced each other to their favourite artists. Dumisani introduced Gogo to Lovemore Majaivana and Solomon Skuza and Gogo furthered his love for Mr Chitungwiza and the Four Brothers. They talked about their future, how Dumisani had written to his family in Bulawayo telling them about their new *makoti* whom he would be bringing to meet them soon. Gogo's family was very fond of Dumisani too. Her mother would ululate and dance around when he came to visit them, call him *mukwasha* and reserve the only sofa for him to sit whilst everyone had to make do with the floor. They would live in Harare but would go to Lupane every holiday. They hoped for two children, a boy and a girl, Rudo and Thando, the names would be different but would mean the same thing. Dumisani would support Gogo in pursuing her passion for nursing and he would pursue his degree in Mathematics. They had planned their future and were both very excited to start their lives in a new Zimbabwe.

It was a Monday, the second week of January 1983, when Dumisani did not turn up for work. Mr. Nyedza asked Gogo about his whereabouts. Gogo did not know. She had last seen him the previous night when they had returned from the bioscope and promised to see each other the next day as they always did. It was not like him to miss work and not tell her if he was unwell. On her lunch break, Gogo went to his house in Chitungwiza, a single-room which was behind the main house. She went straight to the back of the house, checking if anyone else was around. She knocked softly on his door, but no one answered. She rapped, knocked and banged and still no one answered. She went back to work and told Mr. Nyedza she was not feeling well and had to finish early. She then went straight to her house to change and then proceeded to Chiedza's house. She thought maybe one of her many suitors had seen him or heard something.

"He has probably left because *askana*, the way you two fell in love was too quick. *Shuwa* after a month you are talking about marriage and your future? I knew it was too good to be true." Chiedza said, leaning on her door.

"Chiedza, please do not joke around, I am serious. Dumi never acts like this. Do you think any one of your friends might be able to help?" she asked her friend desperately, tears beginning to sting her eyes. Chiedza hugged her friend and reassured her she would ask around and do her best to help her. When Gogo arrived at her house, she found Dumisani sitting by her door, distraught. As soon as he saw Gogo, he stood up and ran to her arms. She embraced him but stepped back when he began to cry. He slowly knelt on the ground, bringing Gogo down with him and began to sob.

"My love, what is it? What is wrong?" Gogo asked as she held him tightly. He sobbed like a child, his face buried in her chest. Each time he tried to say something, he was overcome by emotion and began to sob again. Gogo lifted him and helped him into the house where he sat on her single bed. She made sure he was comfortable then brought him a glass of water which he gulped down before he placed his face in his hands.

"They are killing us. I received a letter from Mama a– and they are killing us. The red berets, they made the– Mama said the– they made Baba dig his own grave before they killed and buried him whilst everyone watched. *Nkosi yami*!" Dumisani sobbed as he narrated the letter back to her whilst she held him, his body jerked from crying.

Gogo held him close and rocked him. It now made sense why Mr Ndlovu would migrate to another country. Their plans would now be altered and she knew they had to think ahead.

"Tomorrow we will plan a way forward. We will leave and maybe go elsewhere," she reassured him, tears teeming down her cheeks. She went out to buy some sadza and chicken from Amai Fadzai's house. She went to the tuck shop and bought a few things they would need when they left. She was ready to leave everything behind and go with Dumi. She was not sure why the red berets were after the Ndebele when they had fought alongside them against the white settlers. *Why would the government want war again when we were still recovering and finding our identity under a new regime? Was democracy a myth? Was freedom a carrot that had been dangled in front of them so they could fight in the liberation struggle?* Gogo pondered on this as she made her way home. When she got to her street, she noticed that the group of children who had been playing *raka raka* in the road were no longer there. It was only 4:00 pm and the streets were already empty. She could only hear the whimpering of dogs running down the road with their tails between their legs.

When she arrived at her room, she found the door wide open, Chitungwiza breathing into her room, sending copies of newspapers and her paperwork flapping about. She threw the groceries she had on the floor and ran into the room to Dumisani. She found her bed flipped over, her four spoons, two forks and a single knife on the floor. Her window had been smashed and there was blood on the windowsill. She saw a tooth on her floor and a trail of blood. She could not make out what had happened. Her heart pounded as she opened her wardrobe and drawers before she went to the back of her room, looking for Dumisani. She began wailing and headed to the main house. She found her landlord locking the door as she approached. He looked at her through the window and pointed down the road.

"They took them there," he whispered, fear lurking in his eyes. She had never seen him that small and defeated. She could not believe that was the man who barked at her when she paid the rent a day late.

"Where? Please, who took him?"

"Them," he said, pointing at his bald head. Gogo could not understand what he meant. She tried to open his door and began shouting. She just wanted to know who had taken Dumi. The landlord closed his window and closed the curtain. Gogo knelt by his door, banging and screaming for him to open and tell her who had taken Dumi. A piece of paper fell from the window. She looked up and saw the landlord standing by the window, pointing at the piece of paper. When he saw her crawling towards the piece of paper, he quickly disappeared.

She could barely see what was written on the piece of paper, but the words sent a chill down her spine. She began to wail, running in the direction her landlord had pointed, the words "red *banditi*" prompting her to move quicker.

***

Chido and Rumbidzo were walking from school when they saw Rumbidzo's father's car pass by. They waved at the car, but his father was looking straight ahead with a cigarette stuck between his lips. The Peugeot 404 farted past them and they ran after it, laughing and shouting Rumbidzo's father's name. They stopped running when the car turned a corner and they could not catch up with it.

"What does *nkhulu* mean?" Chido asked, trailing behind her friend, almost out of breath.

"He is my grandfather, my mother's father. He lives in Lupane," Rumbidzo explained.

"Ok, is *nkhulu* his name?" Chido asked as they turned the corner into their street.

"*Ayehwa*, I do not know his name. Only as *nkhulu*, because my mama comes from Lupane."

"Well, my Gogo comes from Chivhu. That is what baba told me. He said w– " she was interrupted by Rumbidzo's mother who was waving at them, telling him to run faster and get home.

"Are you coming to play later?" Chido asked, waving at her friend, but Rumbidzo did not hear her as he sprinted towards his mother.

When Chido arrived home, she found Gogo outside on the veranda with her knitting. She knelt and greeted her before she went inside and removed her uniform so that she could wash it. It was a Friday, so she had to wash her uniform as soon as she got home. She sat on the floor next to Gogo who sat on her stool, knitting and humming to the song on the radio. Chido tugged at her hair; the cornrows that Gogo had done the previous week had come undone. Chido's lanky frame looked awkward, all her weight on her feet which were tucked under her bottom. Gogo appeared to be worlds away and she did not notice Chido calling her until she touched her cheek with her wet, soapy hand.

"*Yuwi, muzukuru,* what is it?" she uttered as she put her knitting down and wiped her cheek. Chido giggled and sat back down, next to the bucket.

"I have been calling you Gogo, but you were not answering me," she replied, playing with the soapy water.

"What is it? How was school?" Gogo asked, repositioning herself to face her granddaughter. She saw her loose cornrows and thought of the new style she had just seen in the latest *Parade magazine*. Gogo traced Chido's face with her eyes and noticed how much she looked like her father, who looked like his father. The way her nose was long and pointy resembled her mother, but her almond-shaped eyes, full lips, oval jawline and dimples, that was all Garikai, Chido's grandfather. She watched Chido blither about her day, but she was not listening. The way Chido pursed her lips when she sneered reminded her of how her grandfather twisted his mouth when he tried to kiss her. He was not as gentle, lingering and affectionate as Dumisani, but he tried. *Bless his soul.*

"Gogo, do you know why?" Chido asked, staring back at her grandmother.

"Why what?" Gogo asked, realising she had not been paying attention to her granddaughter.

"Googooo, *hamusi kunditerera nhasi*. You are not listening." she said, shaking her head and vigorously scrubbing soap on the pair of socks she had in her hands. Gogo smiled at her and asked her to repeat what she had said. Chido asked her question again.

"Oh, Rumbidzo calls his grandfather *nkhulu*? His mother must be Ndebele then." Gogo replied, going back to her knitting.

"Why are we not Ndebele, Gogo?" Chido asked, still playing with the water.

"Which one is Rumbidzo again? Is it the one with the lazy eye?" Gogo asked. She could never remember the names of all the kids that ran around in their street.

"No, Gogo. He is the one with the missing teeth. Remember I told you about him when you were plaiting my hair," Chido said.

"Oh yes, that one. *Ndamuziva*." she lied. She remembered the day and moment, and she remembered the wave of emotion that had come with telling her granddaughter about her younger self. "It is because there are so many different tribes and Zimbabwe has a variety of them. *Isu tiri ma*Zezuru, your grandfather was a Zezuru."

"Oh, were you ever a Ndebele?"

"No, it does not work like that. You do not just switch it as you switch from speaking Shona to English." Gogo tried to explain it in the best way she could for Chido to understand. "*Asi*, I was almost married to one, once upon a time."

"Why did you not marry him? Was it because you were not Ndebele?" Chido asked. She saw her grandmother give her a *talking eye*. She did not know why she had looked at her like that but she explained how they had learnt about Zimbabwean history at school.

Gogo did not say anything but continued to knit. Her granddaughter's words had evoked pangs of terror and emotion which she had worked hard to bury; how this tribal hatred had led to her losing her true love; how that heartbreak and desperation had driven her into Chido's grandfather's arms. She loved him, cherished and adored him, but she never loved him the same way she loved Dumisani. The love she had and shared with Dumisani was like a ghost, it was something everyone talked about but only a few experienced.

Gogo remembered how, the day she found her room in disarray, the only thought that prompted her to run to Chiedza's house was remembering one of her lovers was a red beret. As luck would have it, it was in the same direction as her landlord had directed her. It did not occur to her that she was still in her pencil skirt that hugged her figure. She pulled her skirt high enough to free her legs, held her shoes and sprinted towards Chiedza's house.

***

Gogo found herself at Chiedza's house. She did not spare the social niceties she usually extended to the old lady who was

Chiedza's landlord. She barged into Chiedza's one room, where she found her on her knees, performing fellatio on her friend. Chiedza was startled and accidentally bit her lover's phallus. The man howled and kneed Chiedza in the face. Gogo froze by the door, not sure who to help first; Chiedza who was on the floor, stark naked with a bleeding nose or the gentleman who was writhing on the floor with his bleeding member in his hands. Gogo threw her shoes on the floor and ran over to cover her friend with a blanket she took from the bed. The man was cursing and trying to stand up.

"Chiedza, you witch! *Wandiruma*. *Yuwi kani*, my member. What will I tell my wife? Is this how you get men to stay? Bite them off and use their blood to make *mupfuwira*? *Hee*!" he shouted, limping towards Chiedza with his hand raised.

"*Iwe*, leave her alone. You should have thought of your wife before you came here. *Buda*, leave this house," Gogo retorted as she stood in front of Chiedza who was wrapping the blanket around her waist and trying to stop her nose from bleeding.

"*Haiwawo*, you whores That is all you know, going after other people's husbands because you are too useless and unsavoury to be wife material," he prated. Before Gogo could turn to see her friend's reaction, Chiedza dashed towards him and hurled the bucket in his face.

"Who are you calling useless?" Chiedza shouted, pulling him by the ear and dragging him towards the door. Her breasts were jerked with every tug on her lover's ear. "Was I useless when you were lying on my breasts and telling me you have never felt man enough until you met me?" The man grabbed the blanket that was wrapped around her waist and tripped her. He tried to jump on to her, but Chiedza kicked him in the chest and he fell on his back. This was not the first time something like this had happened, Gogo now knew not to get involved because knowing her friend, that man would be back in her arms the next day.

Chiedza's landlady came limping on her supporting stick. When she saw her tenant grappling with a man in the nude, without missing a beat, the landlady began to thrash both of them with her stick. Chiedza and her lover stopped fighting and dispersed. She began shouting at them and telling them to leave. Chiedza pleaded with her and tried to explain, but her landlady would not have any of it and limped back to her house. Chiedza rushed into her room and put on the first thing she could find and ran after her landlady. She left her lover to his own devices. Gogo handed him his clothes and he got dressed and hobbled out of the compound.

Gogo was now left alone, looking around the room which was now upside down and her mind raced to her own room and what had made her visit her friend. She began to think about where Dumisani could have been taken and by whom. She hoped that Chiedza would know someone who might have an idea of where Dumisani could have been taken.

Chiedza trotted back into the room and shut the door behind her, then sat on the single bed mattress. The walls of her room were covered with pictures of the new prime minster, Robert Mugabe, of Joshua Nkomo and the other comrades who had brought Zimbabwe to freedom. On the wall behind her bed, she had the Zimbabwean flag hung on the nails which also acted as coat hangers. Chiedza slowly pulled a bra from the Primus stove. She reached for the matches which were on top of the side table next to her bed which also doubled as the kitchen unit and dressing table. Chiedza lit the Primus stove and lit a cigarette.

"Men, you can never please them," she said through her teeth with the cigarette between them. Gogo was still standing in the corner, her mind far away and not paying attention to her friend. Chiedza reached for the packet of rice under her bed and poured it in a bowl. She looked at the tipped bucket on the floor and the small puddle of water, and shook her head. She limped outside, taking the bucket to fetch more water. When she came back, she found Gogo sitting on the bed, crying.

"*Ko askana*, what is it?" she asked, putting the pail of water on the floor and limping to her friend. She sat beside her and embraced her. "I am sure Dumisani is not like that, it is not all men." Gogo began to wail even louder which startled her friend. Chiedza held her as she cried, rocking her, waiting for her to calm down. She envied her friend sometimes, how she was marshalled. Her future seemed secure. She had a man who loved her, who would kill for her, she had a career, she was strong and independent. Chiedza, on the other hand, was not as put together as her friend but that did not mean she wanted to be her. Chiedza was enjoying the freedom that came with independence. Why would she not exercise her freedom and rights as a liberated black woman in a two-year-old Zimbabwe? This had led her to meet Tongai, the soldier who was currently driving her crazy. He was married, but it was not her job to be concerned about that. She had fallen for him without realising it. It could have been the machismo that made her feel safe, but it was also the same thing that repulsed her. This was not the first time they had gone toe to toe. But as much as they had bruised and ravaged each other, mentally, emotionally and physically, they always found their way back to each other. Chiedza could not understand it but again, whoever said love was to be understood. She looked at the red beret that lay on the floor and shook her head. She knew she was going to use that as an excuse to go see him again, but first, she had to console her friend.

"*Chinyarara sha*, what is it? Is this still about what I said or there is something else?" she said. Gogo wiped her tears and blew her nose onto the seam of her pencil skirt. She looked at her friend and narrated what had happened in between sobs. Chiedza went stolid as she processed what her friend was telling her. It became clear what Tongai was prating about earlier today. How the Fifth Brigade, which was an infantry brigade of the Zimbabwean National Army had been trained in North Korea to help the "government" get rid of the dissidents, those who were against ZANU PF under Robert Mugabe. Tongai had gone on to explain how this was a ploy to get rid of the ZAPU which was under Joshua Nkomo.

"They want to get rid of all the Ndebele people because it is believed they betrayed the government." He had said with his head on her bosom and his hand rubbing her thigh.

"Ah, but I do not understand it. Wasn't the white man our common enemy? How has this turned into a tribal thing? Are we not one?" she had asked, gently rubbing his bald head. She slowly traced the scar on his forehead from when bomb shrapnel had cut him.

"It is deeper than that. They betrayed us those descendants of Lobengula. They are conspiring against our leader and we will not stand for it," he had said, turning his head to look at her. "We have already started getting rid of them. We are going to be the early rain clearing the chaff before the spring rains. We will call it Gukurahundi and we will never be a colony again," he had said before he reached to kiss her lips.

"What does this mean for the Ndebele people? Do you not think it is wrong to divide us like that?" Chiedza had exclaimed as she moved her face away from him.

"Well, it is too late now. The government has already deployed soldiers to go into the rural areas and clear them out. They will be doing the same in the cities too." He had slowly pinched her nipple, trying to arouse her.

"Tongai, *urikutii*? What are you saying?" she said, swatting his hand away, "You know my friend's lover is Ndebele and they are planning to move. This cannot be happening. Can you not stop it, it makes no sense?" she had asked, getting out of the bed and reaching for her clothes, preparing to go and tell her friend.

"Chiedza, there is nothing we can do now. Please come back to bed, *sha* I had to tell my wife we got called for a comrades' meeting. I will have to leave soon," he had said, rolling on the bed, unclad, looking at her. "And is your friend not at work right now? Do you really want to stress her out at work hmm? *Huya*." he had crooned, reaching his hand out to her. Chiedza had remained standing by the door. *What difference would a few hours make*? She could not go to Gogo's workplace either, that headmaster was a nuisance. Chiedza slowly began to remove her clothes and joined Tongai in bed, only to be interrupted hours later when Gogo came budging in.

"Did he say anything about where they were being taken?" Gogo asked as she stood up to leave. Chiedza wished she had remembered all this when her friend had come earlier, panicking about Dumisani, but they were not "clearing" in Chitungwiza yet, so he was probably somewhere going about his business.

"No, he did not say. *Asi* we can go and ask him," Chiedza replied, picking up the red beret from the floor.
"Please, let us go now. I need to find him. *Nhai Mwari*, please keep him safe. How can this be happening when we were trying to start our lives in a new Zimbabwe. This is j…" Gogo began to cry. Chiedza turned off the Primus stove and followed her friend.

"Gogo, can I go to Rumbidzo's house and play?" Chido disturbed her grandmother's train of thought. Gogo was startled and it took her a while to come back to the present. Chido had hung her uniform and socks askew on the line. It had taken her a while to hang the uniform as the cable was too high for her. She had also polished her shoes and washed the plate on which she had eaten her lunch whilst Gogo was knitting.

"Yes, you can go but come back early. I do not want to come looking for you again like yesterday. *Wanzwa*?" Gogo warned Chido as she watched her run out of the yard, knowing very well she was going to look for her again because she always lost track of time.

Gogo went inside the house and began to prepare dinner. She boiled meat for the stew and cut the tomatoes and onions. She put a pot of water on the stove and left it to boil, went outside and walked lightly to the back of the house where her vegetable patch was. She picked a few leaves from her kale bunch and pruned the stems. She hummed to herself as she walked back to the house where she washed the vegetables, cut them and put them in with the stewed meat to make a relish. She used the boiled water to prepare the sadza and as it came to simmer, she walked to the door and noticed the sky had turned a purple hue. She peeped at the clock in the kitchen and saw it was past six. Gogo grabbed a cardigan, lowered the heat on the sadza and went out to look for her granddaughter.

When Gogo arrived at Rumbidzo's house, after being directed by a neighbour, she could not see Chido or Rumbidzo playing outside as usual, but she saw someone sitting on a chair on the veranda. As she approached the veranda, she noticed it was an old man. She figured he must be the *nkhulu* Chido had been talking about.

"*Pamusoroi*," Gogo announced, approaching the old man. She watched him look up and their eyes met. He had kind, tired eyes. He looked at her and smiled. His smile disappeared as soon as it had appeared.

"*Makadini henyu*," she greeted him, extending her hand, but the old man stared at her. Gogo slowly lowered her hand and began to look around the compound for Chido. "I am Chido's grandmother and I wanted to ask if you know where she is. She told me she would be here and would be back before dusk, but you know children when it comes to playing," she explained, still looking around, standing next to the old man, but he did not say anything. Gogo concluded he was either deaf or he was not familiar with Shona. So, she thought of speaking to him in Ndebele since Chido had mentioned he was Ndebele.

"*Sthandwa sami*," the old man said before Gogo could utter a word. His words startled Gogo because they were too intimate to say to a stranger. She stepped away from him and cleared her throat. Maybe he had dementia, she thought.

"Ngifun– "

"Do you not remember me," the old man said, standing up and towering over her. She looked into his eyes and saw a familiar sparkle. She could not believe her eyes. She leapt back and held her hands to her chest.

"Dumisani?" she whispered to herself, tears brimming in her eyes.

"Ah, my love. You do remember," he said, walking towards her but the bewildered look in Gogo's eyes made him stop in his tracks and look at her as she processed what was taking place. She looked beautiful; the silver hair and the crow's feet made her look wiser.

"But we buried you, I was there. I mourned you and have been visiting your grave ever since. How could– " she exclaimed, standing against the wall.

"Yes, you did, but that was not me. Let me explain it all to you," he said, gesturing for Gogo to sit down, but she remained standing, hoping her mind was not deceiving her. Dumisani tried to stand, to reach out and talk to Gogo but she turned her back on him and walked away.

The day Gogo had a stroke was the Wednesday after Chamai and Maidei had come back from South Africa. She had been sitting outside, *pamushana*, with her son, when she felt the pain. It started with her face feeling numb, her not being able to lift the corners of her lips to smile, as Chamai told her about South Africa. Her left eye felt heavy, as if the eyelashes were a ton of bricks loaded on her eyelid. She tried to wave at her son, but her arm too, felt heavy. When Chamai realised his mother was not laughing, he turned to her.

"Amai, did you hear me? I said they chased Maidei, until she…" Chamai looked at her. He leapt off the stool as his mother began to keel over. "Amai, can you hear me?" he asked, helping her lie on her back. Gogo did not respond, but her right eye stared at nothing. Chamai called out for his wife and for anyone who would listen.

"Ah, baba, why do you insist on going to see her? You barely know her." Thando said, setting her plate on the table.

"*Indodakazi*, I know her very well. We go way back," Dumisani responded as he dried his hands with the hand towel his daughter had handed him. It had been two days since Dumisani had seen Gogo again. He had tried to visit her, but his daughter had not let him out of her sight since he came. He understood why she insisted on him being at arm's length; he had been feeling unwell and had fallen several times. That was the main reason he had ended up in the hospital twice and had to move from Bulawayo to Harare to stay with Thando. He was not a child who needed to be kept on a leash, but his daughter did not seem to understand. She was just like her mother.

"How baba? Was she a friend of mama?"

"No, she was a friend of mine. From a time when we were still known as the breadbasket of Africa," he said scratching his beard.

"*Hei*! When was that baba? In this Zimbabwe we live in?" she cackled, walking back to the kitchen to get his food. He had been having *isitshwala* and *amasi* because he had lost most of his teeth to old age and from when he fell.

Dumisani slowly ate his food outside on the veranda in front of the house. He liked sitting there and watching the sun set, and in the mornings, he would be there to see it rise again. The orange of the sky and the cool breeze that swept through reminded him of the night he died.

He had been at the back of an Isuzu KB II pickup truck, blindfolded. He had only known of the make of the car because the red beret who had seized him from Gogo's house had been talking about how the new dispensation now owned the latest vehicles because Zimbabwe was free at last.

"*Iwe, todzizivirepi mota dzakadai*? This is a 1980 model, this is the in thing, *wanzwa*!" he said, banging the side of the car. The sound startled Dumisani. There were a number of other people piled into the back of the Isuzu like sacks of maize on their way to the GMB. He could not see anything, but he could hear clearly. With his hands and feet hogtied, he was in a very awkward position. Moving anyhow would make him more uncomfortable or even worse, he could end up on the road with his head cracked open. He heard someone whimpering, another one whispering to their maker and another repeatedly asking "*Ngoba*?"

"Aah, *pfutseke mhani*!" one of the red berets shouted. Dumisani could tell by his staccato that he was Shona, how he pronounced each syllable in *pfutseke* with vim. "You people thought we would not find out about your scheme to take over, *hee*?" No one said anything. The whimperer, the whisperer and the querist all fell silent.

"Now you are quiet? Were you quiet when you were going behind our backs and forming your own party and wanting to take over? *Kutoita misangano* planning on setting us back, were you not tired from the Chimurenga?" His voice was loud, even the wind from the speed of the Isuzu did not drown it out. He spewed about how the Fifth Brigade was on a mission to cleanse the new Zimbabwe of the chaff that was the Ndebele people. He raved about the atrocities they had and would be committing to show loyalty to their land and new regime. Dumisani heard all this as his mind raced to his parents. They were nothing but a memory now. Was he about to be a memory too? Ah! His true love, how was she going to know what had happened to him? Their plans? Their future and the hope of a new Zimbabwe? Tears welled in his eyes as he listened to the red beret soldier narrate how they were going to have them stand side by side in a line and shoot them. Was this how his country would treat him? The country he was serving by passing on his knowledge of numbers to the coming generation? Was all they saw a tribe, not a part of the new Zimbabwe?

They drove for what seemed to be a very long time, going through tarred and dust roads. Dumisani could hear the soldiers talking amongst themselves. At times, they would kick or shout at one of the captives to make a statement.

Dumisani remembered coming to a stop and then being kicked out of the truck. As his eyes were blindfolded, his sense of smell and hearing had heightened. He could smell gasoline and a burning fire and he could hear gunshots and people screaming.

Dumisani shook his head in despair as memories of that day flooded his memory. He was washing his hands after his meal. He took out his small packet of snuff and put a bit under his tongue. Making himself comfortable in his chair and watching the orange sky turn to a deep purple, Dumisani turned on his radio and John Chibadura's *Zuva Rekufa Kwangu* started playing.

Chamai pressed a cold flannel on his mother's face. He silently prayed as he did so, looking at her face, so serene. He traced her cheek with the back of his forefinger. She did not flinch, only the movement of her chest showed she was still one of the living. Chamai wiped his face with the back of his hand. His mother was the last person he had a connection to through blood and water. He had lost his older sister, Rudo to malaria. The way his mother mourned her was etched in his mind. He was only ten when she died, but he remembered seeing his mother cry and lamenting to herself the day of the burial. She had gone to see his sister for the last time before she was buried. He had eavesdropped on her as she said her final goodbye, whilst his father was outside with the other mourners.

"Oh Rudo, my last memento to the life I could have had. *Ndodakazi yami*, your name came from a place of love chosen by the person I loved. He might not have been your father, but you were a carrier of our hope. Oh, you leaving me has awoken new memories that will be buried again with you." She had traced Rudo's cheek with the back of her finger as Chamai did now to his mother. He never got to understand what she had meant, but he was sure he was feeling the same way she had. He was losing a mother and a confidant. He heard a faint knock on the door, loud enough for him to hear but soft enough not to startle him. A familiar face appeared but he could not place the name. He stood up to receive the visitor.

"Baba, *maswera sei*?" Chamai walked towards the visitor and extended his hand for a handshake. He called him baba, as was customary to call an elderly man baba or amai if it was a woman. He later recognised who it was when the old man took off his hat.

"*Litshonile, unjani*?" Dumisani responded, as he waddled into the room with his stick in one hand. His arm stretched towards Chamai, but his eyes raced to Gogo who lay on the bed. She looked more beautiful than before. She had aged but not enough to erase the features that had given him hope to survive so he could see them again. He remembered the mornings he would wake up next to her. She snored softly and always winced her nose before she opened her eyes. He would spend some time looking at her, scrutinising and taking in every part of her face. Her nose, the curve of her chin and at times, the pimple that always appeared on her left cheek when it was near her period.

Chamai had known about Rumbidzo's grandfather through Chido, but had never formally met him. Gogo barely talked about her past, only about how she had met his father and how Zimbabwe was different back then, but she never talked much about the early 1980's. Chamai pumped the old man's hand and cleared the way for him. Dumisani sat on the chair where Chamai had been sitting. Dumisani looked at Gogo as she snored softly, she always let out a soft purr when she snored and Dumisani could not help but smile. It brought back memories of when they lived together. How her snoring had kept him awake many nights, but he could never tell her because he knew she would have refused to spend the night. He found it annoying at times because he would not get enough sleep for him to function at work, but he loved looking at her. He would trace the outline of her face, her lips and kiss her nose before he went to sleep on the sofa. He was feeling an urge to do the same when Chamai cleared his voice.

"I am sorry baba but how do you know my mother?" Chamai had been looking at him from the other side of the room. Dumisani smiled to himself and slowly raised his head to face him.

"She is the love of my life. The reason I am standing here and the reason why my life finally makes sense." He shuffled in his seat and touched Gogo's hand. Chamai looked at him, both confused and amused. He had never thought of another man besides his father to have been his mother's lover. In all honesty, he had never thought about his mother being in a relationship or even being intimate, before or after his father. He only managed to shake his head and laugh. Dumisani laughed with him but looked at him intensely after a while.

"Your mother and I's love has survived aeons of hate, strive and even supposed death. By the look on your face, I can tell your mother never divulged details of her life before you, and I do not blame her. I too never told mine to my offspring but seeing here that there might be no tangible evidence of our love, I guess I might have to tell you, son, my side.

Chamai calmly sat on the bed by his mother's feet. It could have been the fatigue from being up with his mother in the ward for the last twenty hours or it was out of respect for the elderly man, but he sat and listened attentively.

"We met at a time when our tribes were at loggerheads, but we tried to persevere, we tried. You see, I was kidnapped from her house. I am sure you are aware of the atrocities the government committed against the Ndebele, *yebo*?" Chamai nodded. The old man continued telling Chamai about the events of that day.

Dumisani had been dragged out of Gogo's room by the red beret soldiers. Despite the pounding headache and the taste of blood in his mouth, Dumisani remembered how they had hogtied and rummaged through Gogo's house before kidnapping him. He was blindfolded but the smell around him was putrid and heavy. There was the stench of human flesh burning, stale body odour, a whiff of very strong alcohol and the faint sound of a stream or river. They were pushed out of the car and were made to stand in a straight line and the blindfolds were removed from their faces. When Dumisani had his off, he saw about five or six red beret soldiers standing in front of them. His sight was blurry because of the blindfolds, so he could not be sure. They finally saw the face of the man who had been pleading for his life. Dumisani recognised the voice that was muttering for God to save his soul, next to him. He could see the man better as his vision was starting to clear. There were about ten to twelve of them in the line. The man was a short and stocky man and his clothes had been ripped, just like Dumisani's. He did not get a chance to talk to him because before he knew it, the five red berets in front of them were corking their guns. When Dumisani realised what was happening, it was too late. The soldiers began to fire at them and at the point, Dumisani blacked out.

"Ah Baba, how did you survive?" Chamai asked as his hands flew to his mouth.

"*Umfana wami*, even I do not know but when I woke up, I was under the short man and I had an infected leg wound."

"*Eish*, that is something hey. You survived a firing squad?" Chamai asked, shaking his head in disbelief.

"I might have passed out from shock after my leg was shot. That is the only logical thing I can think of. Because how does anyone survive that?" Dumisani said, moving his gaze from Chamai to Gogo, who was still lying peacefully on the hospital bed. "It was a sign that I had a second chance, a chance to find her again and move to a place where we could be free to love and be ourselves." He reached out to hold Gogo's hand and slowly stroked it. "*Kodwa*, it was not to be, until now. I have finally been reunited with *sthandwa sami* after nearly four decades. You see, when I woke up, there was no one, but I had heard they would come back later to burn and bury the bodies. I dragged myself into the forest and I do not know how long I was in there. I was in pain, delirious and lost. I did not know where I was and I was afraid I could be kidnapped again. I survived on wild fruits and water from a river which I followed downstream. I must have passed out because I was later found by a man who had been out hunting. He took me in and helped me get back on my feet."

"Hmm, were you ever afraid that maybe you would be caught again?" Chamai asked.

"Oh yes, I was so paranoid for the first few weeks, but I still wanted to believe in the goodness of people. The man and his family helped me to find a job and nursed me back to health. I can never thank them enough," Dumisani said with tears in his eyes. He was quiet for a while before continuing with his story. "When I had made enough money, I made sure to stay under the radar and went back to Chitungwiza. It was around early 1987 by then, and they had started talking about the Unity Accord. When I got to the house where your mother used to live, she had moved and no one knew where she had gone. I went to her friend, Chiedza's house but she too, had moved. The only information I got was that Chiedza was very unwell and had been in and out of hospital. I continued my search to no avail. It was later on I met Xolie whom I married and had a family with."

"Did she know about your past? About my mother?"

"Oh yes, I told her that I had loved and would always love your mother. She too had a past but that is how it was. I loved her too and she understood." He exhaled deeply and settled in the chair.

"Haa, I can't imagine telling my wife that I love another woman. She would kill me," Chamai said and laughed nervously. His phone rang and he excused himself. When he stepped out, Dumisani began to hum John Chibadura's *Rudo Runokosha,* looking at Gogo's wrinkled hand and stroking it. Gogo flinched and stirred in her sleep. Dumisani looked up and saw that Gogo was looking at him. He stood up as quickly as his rheumatic body would allow him.

"Dumisani," she managed to say, even though she was struggling to keep her eyes open.

"Yes, *sthandwa sami*, it is I. I am here now and will never leave your side again."

Gogo smiled before she became unconscious again. Dumisani kissed her forehead, sat back in his chair and continued humming their song, stroking her hand.

Nyarai

For three months, Nyarai had been standing in front of the mirror every morning. She would turn around from side to side and wonder if there was another way of covering her protruding stomach. She had been tying it since Thursday of the previous week, but it had become painful and uncomfortable. She did so now in front of the wardrobe mirror using her *zambia.*

Taku was sitting in the dining when she came out. He was Mai Mfundisi's fifteen-year-old son. He had his father's big, bright eyes and bushy eyebrows.

"*Sisi* Nyarai, I am hungry. Make me something to eat," he said. "Mama said you should be done cooking by seven o'clock because there is a prayer meeting tonight. Don't forget to polish my shoes and pack my bag. Tomorrow I am being made a prefect and I have to look presentable," he added, dropping his bag on the marble dining table and leaving to go to his room.

"Yes, *mukoma* Taku." She walked into the kitchen where the dishes from lunch and a note with the menu for the dinner were waiting for her. She made Taku a PB and J sandwich and called him to tell him it was ready. She began to take out the pots and the ingredients for the dinner.

"Nyarai!" Taku shouted from his room, "why are you not bringing the sandwich to me? You know how I hate pausing my games. What would you know about online games? No wonder Mama says you are useless." He stomped into the kitchen, took the sandwich and slammed the kitchen door as he went out. Nyarai pretended not to hear him and continued to peel the potatoes at the sink. When she turned around to get the fresh cream from the fridge, she saw Mfundisi standing next to the fridge, looking at her.

"*Maswera sei* Mfundisi?" she said, curtsying in front of him.

"Hmm Nyarai, there is no need for you to be doing all that. Come give daddy a hug. *Hee.* Come, I have missed you *shaa*," Mfundisi said, walking towards her and stretching his arms to hug her.

"No." She pushed him back. "*Mukoma* Taku is here, I don't want him to catch us. He almost did the last time." She went back to the sink and continued to peel the potatoes. Mfundisi walked towards her and put his hands around her waist. Nyarai dropped the potato she was peeling together with the peeler and rested in his embrace.

"I need you to stop calling that boy *mukoma*. He is six years younger than you for goodness' sake. Doesn't he know you are carrying his little brother or sister? And do not worry, I saw him going out to see his friend and also sent him to the shops, so we can spend some time together." Mfundisi rubbed Nyarai's belly. She was six months along but anyone who did not know her could not tell she was pregnant. She placed her hands on top of Mfundisi's and smiled.

"But daddy, when are we going to tell people about us? I cannot keep tying my stomach and soon that slow wife of yours will catch on," she asked, cosying up to him and kissing him. "People need to know I am the real first lady of the church. That Mai Mfundisi title is mine and you need to start doing something because our child is due in less than three months." Nyarai freed herself from Mfundisi's arms and walked towards the fridge for the fresh cream.

"Honey, I know how you feel and I agree. Hmm, but you know with me being the pastor, it takes time and I need to be careful of my reputation. I also need to know Taku is taken care of when I decide to divorce his mother."

"Decide? Aah, what do you mean, decide?" She looked at him with her hands on her hips.

"Lameck, what are you saying?" She walked towards him and just as she was about to poke his head with her finger, Mai Mfundisi came through the kitchen door. Mfundisi looked at his wife and at Nyarai. He then pretended he had been telling Nyarai off.

"See these plates Nyarai? They are ceramic, not *zenge* which you are used to in the rural areas. Do you hear me?" He walked towards his wife to kiss her.

"Ah daddy, I have told her that before, but I guess you can take the girl out of the rural areas but not the rural out of the girl," she sneered and kissed her husband.

"How was your day my love?" Mfundisi asked as he escorted his wife to the dining room and winked at Nyarai who was in the kitchen behind him. After they left the kitchen, Nyarai stood there, teeming with anger. She collected herself and began making the scalloped potatoes.

"*Iwe* Nyarai!" Mfundisi shouted from the dining room. "Make my wife a cup of tea with no sugar please. She is sweet enough." Nyarai heard them laugh from the kitchen.

"Yes Mfundisi" Nyarai put the kettle on and prepared the tea for Mai Mfundisi. When she was at the door, about to enter the dining room, Nyarai spat in the tea. She smiled and said to herself,

"All this will be mine soon." She took the tea to Mai Mfundisi, whom she found sitting on the couch.

"My love," he said, kissing his wife's forehead, "Let me go and freshen up. I will come join you for Bible study." He trotted out of the dining room and as he was passing Nyarai, he fondled her buttock. Nyarai staggered but did not say anything.

"Set the tea over there and hand me my handbag." Mai Mfundisi put her feet up on the foot stool. Nyarai moved towards the coffee table but stopped in her tracks. Mai Mfundisi went on, "Where is Taku? Is everything set for tomorrow? People need to see that he comes from a house with parents who are there for him. You know? Who lead by example like we d– Haah *iwe* Nyarai, why are you just standing there?" she kissed her teeth, turning to face Nyarai who kept standing there, the cup of tea shaking in her hand. She let out a loud yelp and fell on the floor. Mai Mfundisi rolled her eyes and muttered to herself. "Now what is this nonsense? You better not die in my house please." She slowly peeled herself from the couch. She knelt next to Nyarai's unconscious body and nudged her, but Nyarai did not move. She felt for a pulse but could not feel anything. Nyarai was sweating yet cold to the touch. Mai Mfundisi called for her husband, standing up and reaching for her cup of tea to take a sip. Mfundisi came down, humming and grinning from ear to ear. "Yes, my love? Are you enjoying your t–" He rushed over to Nyarai who lay on the floor.

"And what happened? Did she fall? Nyarai, wake up." He frantically shook Nyarai, trying to sit her up. "Iwe," he turned to his wife who had made herself comfortable on the couch, ignoring her frantic husband. "*Are* you seriously watching T.V? Have you no heart? Call the ambulance or something. Did you do somet–"

"Ah ah ah. Lameck, shut up. You think *I* did something to her when you two have been gallivanting and playing house? In my house! You think I do not know what has been happening here? You think I am blind *handiti*?" She pointed at her eyes which were still staring at the T.V and sucked her teeth. "You and your concubine can carry each other or whichever way. Make sure you get out of my house." She took another sip of her tea and looked at her watch. She then turned to look at her husband trying to carry Nyarai who was groaning lightly and had now opened her eyes slightly.

"Please hurry. It's almost time for my cell group and I hope she had finished sorting out the food. I saw you *hangu* through the window, caressing each other and telling each other sweet nothings." Mai Mfundisi laughed to herself, still focusing on the T.V. "I will leave you to continue. Who am I to stand in the way of you two being there for each other in sickness and in health?"

"Pamela, please. I am sorry but come help me here. Do you want her to die here? Does the Bible not say to help those… eh… in need? Act like a pastor's wife, *wanzwa*?" he said, trying to remain balanced with Nyarai in his arms. Mai Mfundisi got up from where she was sitting and left the two of them. Nyarai's breath was now staggered and she was sweating. Mfundisi kept calling her name, but she was not responding, only groaning and breathing labouredly.

Mfundisi set Nyarai on the sofa and when he put her down, he noticed blood on his hand. He scanned her body to see if she had hurt herself when she fell. He noticed her *zambia* was wet and realised what had happened. A trail of blood mapped where she had fainted to the sofa where she now lay, barely breathing.

"Pamela! Come he– Oh lord, plea– Nyarai, *muka*. Nyarai, open your eyes. You need to wake up!" he cried, shaking her and keeping an eye on the door his wife had exited. Nyarai was lapsing in and out of consciousness and her breath was raspy.

"What? Lameck, I am not doing this with you again. *Wanzwa*? Do you remember you said the last two maids were the last ones? You made a joke out of me, Lameck huh? All the ladies from church know about your shenanigans. Did you even think about me?" Mfundisi could hear her through the door. "I am tired. I cannot put on a brave face and be a 'good' wife. I am leaving and you will have to explain to Taku." She came into the dining room carrying a small suitcase and a handbag. She saw the huge patch of blood and looked at Mfundisi, who was now crying over Nyarai's body. She looked at her husband, then at Nyarai's lifeless body, shook her head and carried her suitcase out through the door.

"Ah, Amai. We were just about to knock. I hope you had not forgotten about the ladies meeting. You lo– *Hezvo*. Amai, are you packing?" Mai Chipata asked, standing by the door as Amai Mfundisi calmly pushed her suitcase to the car. The other ladies who were with her all craned their heads, trying to see what was happening and whispering behind Mai Chipata. Taku came into the yard and asked his mother why she was leaving. Amai Mfundisi silently walked towards him, hugged him then got into her car and drove away. The ladies all stood at the door, looking at each other, trying to make sense of what had taken place. Taku walked into the house and the ladies trailed behind him.

They all gasped when they saw Mfundisi crying over Nyarai's dead body.

3:15 AM

Previously published in
Brilliance Of Hope - an anthology of short stories compiled and edited by Samantha Vazhure.

3:15 AM

I have been waking up at 3:15 am every day for the last five months, and each time my eyes open, I see her. I lie on my back and stare at the ceiling in the dark. I feel her glare, following me as I toss and turn. There is barking and growling outside my window, I think they are dogs, but I could be wrong. I tend to only hear them when she visits. She does not move but stares at me. She looks exactly the same as she did on that day back in 2002. It has been over 17 years since she died, but I can still hear her singing on our way to the river like it was yesterday. I have told Mama about how she has been visiting me, wearing the same clothes as that day, staring at me the same way she did as she took her last breath on that day, but I do not tell her the last part. Mama tells me it is because I miss her and she recalls how close and inseparable we were, but I remember it differently and I do not tell her.

I get up, put my bedside slippers on, a gift from Aunt Saru. I turn on my bedside lamp and I see her standing in front of me. I no longer freeze in terror or panic when I see her. We have become acquainted again. We do not talk, but our silence speaks volumes. I check the clock on my wall, 3:17 am, 3 more minutes until she leaves. I look at my phone, but I do not take it. The first time she visited me I tried to use my phone to call, but before I could even unlock it, I could not move and words would not escape my mouth. It happened again the following day when I tried to use it as a torch. I guess this is her way of telling me she needed my undivided attention. She was like that before she died, self-centred and commanded attention in every room she walked into. I shuffle to the door and pat my way in the dark to turn on the light as I head to the kitchen.

It is too late for wine and too early for coffee, so I put the kettle on and open the cupboard for a tea bag. There is no barking or growling. I take milk out of the refrigerator and open the bottle. I pour the last of the milk in my mug, hot water, a dash of honey then I put the teabag. The hairs at the back of my neck stand and that is how I know she has joined me in the kitchen. The usual flickering of lights and the flapping of the cupboard and drawers no longer shocks me. I am surprised that fear no longer suffocates me as before. She always takes longer to make her way downstairs. I think she will be giving herself a tour, taking a glimpse of what her life might have been like if she were still alive. I hear growling outside my kitchen window. I drag my feet to my kitchen bin and throw away the teabag. I sit on the kitchen chair and she sits opposite me. Her pale grey skin makes her look ghostly, but again, she is. I smile at her, but she vehemently stares back at me. She does not smile or flinch, just a straight line that is neither a smile nor a frown. That was how her lips looked too on the day she died.

My cousin Rukudzo and I were born a few months apart, and our mothers always bought us matching clothes. People used to think we were twins even though they said she was prettier and lighter than I was. She had big, upturned eyes, a carefully carved wide nose, full lips and smooth skin. I, on the other hand, did not possess her features of beauty, or what society deemed an acceptable standard. Even though my mother told me I was beautiful the way I was, I was always the other. Every school holiday, my parents, my older sister Sarudzai, named after Rukudzo's mother, and I would head down to Chivhu, in Njanja where we spent the holidays. There, we would meet Aunt Saru, Uncle Takura, Rukudzo and her little brother Kupakwashe. Gogo and Sekuru always enjoyed having us over, but I never enjoyed it. I always dreaded it. My grandparents always marvelled at how Rukudzo was already able to cook a big pot of sadza, enough for eight people at the age of ten. She would wash our grandparents' clothes at the river all by herself and was able to balance a 7.5-litre clay pot on her head. No one would pay attention to how I had come first in my class or how I was reading at Grade 7 level, even though I was in Grade 5. No one even acknowledged I was almost as tall as Sarudzai, who was 4 years older than me.

It was the last Sunday of the holiday. I remember it distinctively because we had come from church and Gogo had instructed Sarudzai to kill a chicken for dinner. The last Sunday was the only time my grandmother would have a chicken killed for food. She kept them for selling and to pay debts when push came to shove. Sekuru had given me his pair of trousers, shirt, and socks which he had worn for church and asked me to wash them for him before we left.

"I would love it if you washed these for me muzukuru," he said as his adam's apple bobbed up and down his wrinkled throat. "You are a big girl now and I know you will manage these." he said, handing me the clothes. I loved how he saw me and acknowledged me. He could have asked Sarudzai or Rukudzo, but he asked me and that made me happy. I took the metal bucket which had accumulated a little rust, a small piece of Elangeni soap and made my way to the river which was not far from the house. I walked past Sarudzai and Kupa who were chasing the chicken around the yard to no avail. I remember laughing at Kupa who was running towards the kitchen when the chicken ended up chasing him. I walked down to the river, humming to myself. I was going to make Sekuru proud.

"Wait!" I heard Rukudzo shouting behind me. I ignored her and increased my pace.

"I know you can hear me. Wait!" She continued. I stopped in my tracks and waited for her to catch up. I had wanted to go alone so I could make Sekuru proud and show everyone that I could also wash clothes as good as Rukudzo, if not better. She caught up and stood next to me catching her breath. The red pendant on her necklace had moved to the back, she repositioned it and grinned at me.

"Ko why did you ignore me? Did you not hear me calling you?"

"No." I lied.

"Oh, inga. Maybe there is something wrong with your hearing because I was shouting loud enough for the whole village to hear."

"Well, maybe it wasn't as loud as you thought."

"Anyway, where are you going? You know we are not allowed to go down to the river without an adult accompanying us," she remarked, sizing me up and down. I was an inch taller than she and I knew it gnarled her that I was better than her at something.

"Sekuru said I was big enough to go by myself and wash his clothes." I said standing up taller, sticking my chest out, rubbing my stature in her face.

"Kunyepa, sekuru would never say that. You are lying. I will go and ask him," she said, threatening to run back home and ask.

"Go ask him," I replied, as I continued walking down to the river with the bucket under my arm. I did not hear any footsteps fading or approaching me, so I knew she was standing, digesting my words.

I was hoping she would go back home and leave me alone, but a moment later, I heard her walking behind me, singing to herself. She had the most beautiful voice I had ever heard, but I would never tell her that. Her head would grow too big and she would tell it to everyone who would listen. I ignored her and quickened my steps, but she picked up her pace, she was so close I could feel her breath when she sang. As I made my way to the ruware, the riverside dwala where we washed our clothes, Rukudzo hurried beside me and snatched the bucket out from under my arm. I tried to chase her but she was too quick for me and the ruware was very slippery.

"Give me back my bucket, Rukudzo! Hunza kuno!" I shouted after her as tears itched my eyes." Come back and give it to me, now!"

"Oh, don't be a cry baby. I am saving you. I don't want you to embarrass yourself apa." She retorted, taking out the clothes from the bucket.

"Rukudzo, give it back or I will beat you up!" I had never fought a day in my life, except playing the slap game with Sarudzai, which I never won, but that day I was willing to defend my honour. I was not going to let her win.

"Eheeeeeeede, you beat me?" She cackled and clapped her hands three times. She narrowed her eyes and looked at me as I stood a short distance from her. "Try me. Let us see if you will be able to talk when I finish with you." She said, taking off her shoes and tucking her yellow dress into her knickers. I was taller but not stronger and seeing that I was never going to overpower her, I decided to make use of the resources around me.

"Come and beat me," I said, holding a huge rock in my hand. If push came to shove, I was prepared to use it.

"Zigwara, you are such a coward. We both know I am better than you. Even your own sister said it too. You can't even defend yourself but need something else to defend you." She retorted looking me straight in the eye, but I did not flinch.

"You are lying, Sarudzai would never say that!" I shot back, trying not to cry.

"Oh really, so how do I know you don't know how to wash your own knickers yet? Huh, how would I know that? Tell me!" She jeered and laughed louder than her usual cackle. That set me off. Sarudzai knew I had been having a hard time washing my whites and she knew I was getting better. How could she betray me like this? I ran towards Rukudzo, not paying attention to the slippery rock and stood in front of her. Her toes were touching my shoes and I could feel her warm breath enveloping my nose.

"What? What are you going to do about it?" she asked, pushing me hard with her finger, but I did not budge.

"Give me the bucket," I said, standing my ground. I could feel the brim of my eyes itching, but I was not going to let her use my tears against me. I had to win this time.

"Take it, but rest assured you will have to go past me." She blocked me from the bucket. I leaned forward to grab the bucket and before I could grab the handle, a sharp pain spread on my cheek. I retreated my hand and held my cheek as Rukudzo pushed me and slapped my head. The tinnitus that followed confused me. I could not make sense of what was happening. By the time I came to my senses, Rukudzo had started washing Sekuru's clothes. I stood up and walked towards her. She had her back at me and was humming to herself. The nerve of her not turning her back and not being afraid of what I could have done to her annoyed me. Did she not think I was threatening enough?

"Rukudzo" I said, poking her shoulder. Seeing that I had been defeated, trying to fight her would end with me limping back home, so I opted for a civil approach. She stood up and as she was turning to face me, she slipped and fell into the river. She was on the shallow end and she tried to grab on to the rocks, but they were too slippery. She called out my name and I rushed to the riverbank. She grappled with the strong currents that were threatening to sweep her away. I held out my hand and when she was about to get a hold of it, I hesitated and pulled it back. She screamed my name and called for help as the water overpowered her. I stared at her as she wrestled with it. I waited for her to fight the water the same way she wanted to fight me. She had told me last holiday that she could swim, so I left her to her own devices.

She stared at me, the same stare she gives me when she visits. She gave in to the current and was swept away before I could reach out to grab her hand. I ran back to the house, shouting and screaming for help. It had just dawned on me that Rukudzo could not swim. Uncle Takura and my father ran towards me as I shouted for help. They came running towards me, but I could not speak. I only managed to point in the direction of the river. They ran towards the river and seeing how I kept looking to the east where the river flowed, Sekuru hobbled with his stick in that direction. By the time they found her, she was already dead, and her stomach was bloated, full of water. When they brought her home, Sekuru could not let me and Kupa near her, but I saw a glimpse of her face. Her blank stare pierced through my eyes and I have lived with that image in my head for the past 17 years. Even after we moved to London, I could still see her face when I closed my eyes, but it had begun to fade with every new face I saw every day. I guess her visiting me every day at 3:15 am, is a way of not wanting me to forget her.

I sip on my tea and stare at the clock. 3:21 am. the barking and the growling have stopped again. Silence. She is gone. I rinse my cup and carefully place it on the rack. I survey the kitchen to see if she is still around, but I am reassured of her absence by the flat hairs at the back of my neck. I make my way upstairs and get into my bed. I coil up, make myself comfortable and close my eyes, certain that tomorrow at 3:15 am, Rukudzo will pay me another visit.

Chipo

I held her hand as she lay on the bed, snoring softly. I took in every inch of her face; her glowing skin, the once long and bouncy curls that were now patches on her oval shaped head. I traced her nose which I kissed each morning before she woke up, the full lips which produced malicious words when her brilliant brain could not solve a problem or when I could not understand what she meant, even after she had explained it to me numerous times, the lips I loved to kiss, the ones that uttered 'I love you' first before I was ready to say it.

I won't lie, I was taken aback by her boldness. Not because I did not know I loved her, but because I was so used to the typical Zimbabwean girls who showed their feelings by being passive aggressive. Chipo was different. She knew what she wanted and she was never afraid to speak her mind. She made me uncomfortable with her forwardness. Her resilience and mental agility kept me wanting to unveil her for my own understanding. She was a breath of fresh air, although she suffocated me sometimes. I cannot say I have ever fully known or understood her. She cannot be defined by one word. She is both an introvert and extrovert, shy and outspoken, kind and selfish, sweet and has the temper of a two-year-old. She kept me on my toes and I loved that. I still love it.

As I sit here, seeing her weather away, I cannot help but think God is playing a cruel joke on me. I cannot stop thinking about the time I wasted looking for something I already had. I cannot stop thinking about the first day I met her.

It was a blind date. Mazvita had set us up. I had known Mazvita liked me for a very long time, but I never engaged. I do not know if she set me up with Chipo because she genuinely wanted me to find someone or she was subtly telling me that she wanted me by making *this* move. Surprisingly, Chipo and I got along quite well. I took her out for ice cream. It was May, but summer was still very much around although the breeze was cooler. She wore a dusty pink top that shaped her torso, a red maxi skirt and yellow pumps. Her hair – God, her glorious hair – was big and free. I could not stop looking at her. At first, she seemed a little shy, but as I got to know her more, I realised it was not that she was shy, but she was studying me.

"Tonde, you don't just start yapping about new people. You study them, sense their energies, then you engage," she told me when we started dating. On our first date, I did all the talking. She asked questions here and there. My occupation, how I knew Mazvita and other basic things. We sat on a bench in Africa Unity Square. A bit cliché, yes, but I did not know where to take her. She licked her ice cream and observed people in the park. Just across us, there was a couple who were having pictures taken. They were posing awkwardly, the lady was trying to sit on her lover's legs, but they were too short to support her bountiful bottom. We both involuntarily laughed and looked at each other.

"So, how is *this* going for you so far?" she asked me. I was not having the best time, but I was comfortable. I was not really feeling anything, frankly. She was attractive, yes -

smart and creative, but I did not have a flutter in my chest or sweaty palms. I was planning to drop her off at her house, delete her number and try my luck elsewhere.

"Well, it's fun. Nothing beats sitting next to a beautiful lady and eating ice cream in a park," I said, trying to charm her. She did not look amused.

"Hmm, so you think there is going to be a second date?" she asked me calmly, looking into my eyes. I was uncomfortable and to top it off, I was about to lie, which I am very bad at. I remember chuckling and looking away. *What is going on here?* I thought to myself. I had never been with a girl who was so direct. I was used to girls who would shy about and just do what they thought I wanted. They seemed to want to please me more than to also be pleased, but this one was different, and I was not equipped to deal with this kind of charm.

"Ehm, yeah, yeah. Of course," I stammered, which made her laugh. I was confused but I laughed with her. The way she threw her head back when she laughed caught my attention. She laughed with the freedom of a child.

"You do not have to lie. I can tell you are not particularly enjoying this." I just smiled. I was at a loss for words. I licked on my ice cream, which was dripping on my hand, praying for this awkward moment to pass.

"I am looking for consistency, respect, honesty and fun. What about *you*?" She asked me as if we had known each other for the longest time. Like we had got to the stage of calling each other by childhood nicknames, yet it was just our first date.

"Ok, uhm, I value openness, sense of humour and stability," I said.

"Haa! Did you just say the same things I said using different words?" she laughed, shaking her head.

Touché, she had caught me.

"Well, haha…" I was at a loss for words once again. She had called my bluff. She was studying me.

"Ok, I will give you another chance. Tonderai, what are *you* looking for? You know…using your own words this time. Not copying or twisting other people's words," she said as she flashed her carefully arranged teeth. She had– she *has* a pretty smile.

"Alright, alright. I see what you did there. You are mocking me, aren't you." I am not proud to admit it, but I was blushing. She had made me blush. One could never tell but the dumb grin on my face betrayed me.

We walked in silence to my car which I had parked a few metres from Herald House. As we approached the car, I went over to open the door for her. However, the City Council had other plans for me. They had clamped my car because of a speeding ticket I had forgotten to pay for. She had left her car parked at home due to the fuel shortage that had now become the norm. She looked at me and shrugged. "Kombi, I guess." she said as she closed the door. I smiled at her sheepishly, embarrassed. The fact that we had to walk in silence again did not appeal to me. She, on the other hand, did not appear moved by the fact that we had to walk from Second Street to Copacabana where she boarded her kombi. From my history with Zimbabwean girls, a car was what made you graduate from a "maybe" to a "definitely." "Do not worry, I understand how hard adulting is. Trust me," she said as we walked past Angwa Street. It was rush hour. Harare was at its peak with cars hooting, drivers shouting and *hwindis* cussing in defence of their drivers' manoeuvring. I walked close to her, partly to protect her from the pickpockets and waifs who now prowled the streets hoping for a score, but mostly so I could smell the scent of lavender that wafted around her.

I do not know why I boarded the *kombi* with her, but in a few minutes, we headed to Westgate where she lived. Our silence was filled by the raspy voice of Oliver Mtukudzi as he lamented *Pindurai Mambo* through the speakers of the *komb*i. Being the gentleman I am, I paid for the both of us. She was a bit hesitant, but she let me pay. She sat by the window, and I was wedged between her and a lady who was talking on the phone tumultuously. It was as if she was in a tug of war with Mtukudzi, competing over who could be the loudest. We alighted at Westgate Shopping Mall and began to walk towards her house. She told me about her childhood, growing up an only child and how she was close to her family. She told me how sceptical she was about moving into her own place, but she had got used to it now, how she came to discover she loved art and how she was planning on making paintings that would be exhibited in some of the most popular galleries and museums.

"Even at the Louvre!" she exclaimed, standing in front of her door, her keys clutched in her hands. I was amazed by how she talked about painting and art, how her eyes widened and brightened, the excitement in her voice when she told me about her favourite artists and their patterns. I loved how she lost herself in her imagination as she explained how art had been her escape. We were bonding. We were past the awkward stage.

"This is me," she said, pointing at her door as if we had not been standing in front of it for the last twenty minutes. She looked at me and smiled. She moved closer and leaned forward. After our bonding session and her teasing me earlier, I thought I was in and I kissed her.

"What do you think you are doing!" she exclaimed as she moved away from me.

"Well, you leaned in and I thought yo…" I tried to explain myself. I had misread her leaning in as her wanting to kiss me.

"Well, you thought wrong. I only kiss my husband *wanzwa*? I do not understand how you though…"

So she had been leaning in for a hug.

"Hold on! Husband? You are married and you had me take you out on a date in broad daylight?"

"No! I mean to say I am…well…I was saving my first kiss for my husband, now I… *mxm* actually, please leave," she snapped at me as she struggled to unlock the door.

"Wait, aren't you like twenty six and you are telling me you have never kissed anyone?" I asked her, making sure I hadn't misunderstood her.

"Please leave."

"Wait," I persisted, holding the door which she was about to shut in my face. "Help me understand. You said you were saving your first kiss for your husband. Where is he?" I could not fathom what she was saying. Was she in an open marriage? Was her husband Jesus? I had so many questions.

She looked at me for what seemed to be the longest time then heavily sighed. "Ok, the thing is, I made a vow to God that I would wait until marriage to have an intimate physical connection with anyone." She said it so confidently and so matter-of-factly. I do not know why, but I laughed. I had never heard anything like that before. *She was one of those girls who used such tactics to play hard to get,* I thought. She sneered and before I could explain myself, she slammed the door in my face. I knocked, but I was reassured this was how the night was going to end by the key I heard turning behind the door. I stood outside her door trying to explain myself for a good ten minutes, but the only response I got was her turning off the light on the porch where I was standing. With that, I knew she was not coming out.

I won't lie, I was annoyed. The whole trip from Westgate to town, leaving my car on Second Street and walking all the way to Fourth Street to get a *kombi* home to Msasa Park had been for nothing. I remember calling Mazvita to tell her how sensitive and uptight her friend was. "I know you were trying to help and all, but please do not set me up with any of your friends," I told her as I stood in the middle of my living room, shouting at the top of my voice.

"Wow, she really did a number on you, huh?" Mazvita said at the other end of the line.

"She is just… I don't even know what to say." I was not very sure why I was so annoyed. Was it because she had not played to the beat of my drum or because she was hard to read? I too was a bit confused by how irritated I was by the whole ordeal. I thought of texting her and speaking my mind, but I got a hold of myself. She had made it clear she wanted nothing to do with me, so I also wanted nothing to do with her.

"Ah, so if you don't want me to set you up with my friends, *pasara inini*," Mazvita cooed on the other end of the line. I barely paid attention to her, my mind still trying to perceive what had happened earlier.

"Haha, Mazvita *so*. You know you are like a sister to me. You will always be my girl, but these your friends. Please, no."

For two months, I went on with my life. I did not try to contact Chipo to ask about her whereabouts, but I could not stop thinking about her. I could not stop replaying the images of her smile, thinking about her free afro. Her gentle, confident air haunted my mind. I tried to go on dates with other girls, tried to engage with them but I found them lacking something. They all talked about how they wanted to please their man and do whatever he wanted.

"What do *you* like? What are *you* looking for?" I wanted to ask. I stopped going on dates and decided to be the bigger person and text Chipo. She had told me to leave her house but not her. So, I still had a chance there. I had to know why she was still on my mind, even after I had blocked her on all the social media platforms to restrict myself from stalking her.

It was a Saturday morning when I texted her. I had nothing planned for the day, so I had all the time to plan out my strategy and find a way to make things work in my favour. I did a few push-ups and lunges before I texted her. I do not know why, but I felt like I needed to be ready for anything.

She blue ticked me and never replied. I spent the day playing Fifa and checking my phone. I decided to be more intentional because I knew texting would not get me anywhere. For all I knew, she could have already blocked my number. I decided to go to the Art Exhibition at the Rainbow Towers where Mazvita had told me Chipo was showing her art pieces.

I saw her standing by one of her pieces. It was a painting of a man, big and strong, his muscles looking as if they were about to pop out of the canvas. He was shielding a woman from what seemed to be a falling building. The woman was putting a crown on the man's head. I could see that the painting told a story. Chipo had her hair tied in a huge bun, which looked amazing on her. She had on a white shirt and black cigarette pants that traced her every curve and black open-toe sandals. She looked beautiful.

I waited until she had finished her exhibition and when people had displaced. She was packing her things, completely unaware of my presence. I stood behind her for a solid three minutes, thinking of what to say.

"Need any help?" I blurted out, moving in clear view. She looked up at me and sighed.

"Oh, it's you. You have come back to laugh at me again?" she shoved the remaining pieces in her carry case. She had a funny expression on her face. Her lips were tight and her eyes opened wide. I could not tell if she was being sarcastic or serious. I did not want to take any chances.

"No. Please, hear me out. I am so sorry for laughing. That was stupid of me. Truly. Let me make it up to you." I meant it. I could not get her out of my mind. I had to know why I was so drawn to her, why a 30-year-old man lay awake in the middle of the night, thinking of what to say to a woman he had only met once.

"And if I say no?" she asked, looking at me. Her confidence made me nervous.

"Well, I will keep showing up."

"You know that is called stalking, right?" she said, her head tilted slightly. .

"Ok, will you give me another chance, please? We can go anywhere you want, but let me make it up to you."

"Hmm, anywhere you say?" she asked, her arms crossed over her chest, with her index finger tapping her chin.

"Yes, anywhere."

"Ok, next Sunday you can come to my church."

"Ok, cool. You go to New Life right?"

"That is correct."

"Ok. That will be alright. First service, second or the third one?"

"All of them, I guess," she said, shrugging. I did not want to protest the idea of attending all three services of which the first started at 7 am, the second at 11 am and the last one at 3 pm. I just nodded.

She took her bags and walked towards me. I straightened up and looked at her.

"Just so you know, I am stretching my hand so we can shake hands. I am not leaning in for a kiss, ok?" She said it with a smile on her face. I laughed as I also stretched my hand to shake hers which was soft. I walked her to her car and helped her load her things.

I did not contact her the days prior to our meeting. When Sunday finally came, I arrived at the church at around 6:50 am and found seats that were not too close to the pulpit. I texted to tell her I had arrived and had saved her a seat. She replied and asked me to look behind the pulpit. When I turned my gaze towards the pulpit, and I saw her sitting amongst people who wore the same colour clothes as her. She was in the choir. She smiled and waved at me as she was fixing her microphone. I did the same and took my Bible off the seat I had reserved for her and placed it on my lap. Well played, I thought to myself. This girl was putting me on a test to see if I was serious or not. She was going to be singing at all three services, which meant I would only see her after 5 pm. Challenge accepted, I said to myself. What harm could come from listening to the gospel for the whole day? I sat through the first service quietly, listening to the pastor who was talking about the joy of the Lord. During the second service I paid more attention and even took the time to turn to my neighbour and reassure them their blessing was around the corner. By the third service, I was standing with the church mothers who hollered "Hallelujah" and "*Hameni*" when the pastor prophesied that we were no longer slaves of fear but children of God, or that victory was already ours. I had even forgotten about Chipo.

Afterwards, we had an early dinner and talked about the services. I told her about how the church mothers reminded me of my mother who had died of cancer a few years back, how she always stood in the church throughout the service, shouting hallelujahs and amens back to the pastor.

"I am sorry about your mom," she said as I walked her to her car after dinner.

"It's alright. Such is life hey," I said. "Thank you for inviting me to your church. I really enjoyed the services."

"No problem. You should come again," she said, opening her car door and getting in.

"Yeah, sure. Definitely," I replied, closing the door for her.

"I guess this is goodnight," she said and started her car.

"Yeah, I guess it is. Goodnight." I thought she was going to say something else, but she closed her window and drove off.

I stood in the parking lot dumbfounded. This girl had brought me to the church, which I enjoyed, but she had barely said anything regarding us. I knew there was not much, but leaving me hanging like that was just cruel. As I was walking to my car, I heard a car slowing down beside me.

"Hey." It was Chipo.

"Hey," I responded, not sure what else to say.

"Are you free next Saturday? I have an exhibition at the Meikles Hotel, and I would love it if you came," she said looking out her window. I was still walking but a bit slower now. I tried to come up with a quick quip to make her laugh, but I could not think of any.

"I would love that," I responded.

"I would love that too," she said, then slowly drove by me to my car. We bid each other goodbye, both in our cars. And from that day, it was smooth sailing.

***

We had our ups and downs. I remember the other day when she annoyed me. I am hardly a person who holds grudges, but at times she got on my last nerve. I wanted to talk to her and text her all day, but I had to stand my ground.

I know it was petty, but I saw my chance and grabbed it. We would later laugh about it when I told her.

I courted her for eight months before I proposed. If I am being frank, I took that long because I did not want it to seem as if I was rushing her, but I had been ready from the time we went on our third date. We would go out every Saturday night after her choir practise. We met each other's friends and families. We spent most of our time with our friends, but Friday night was our day. After our 9-to-5's, we would meet and choose a restaurant to go to or watch a movie. At times, we made no plans on Saturdays and would drive in any direction and just explore the country. We made sure not to spend too much time apart. The day I asked her to be my girlfriend, she had told me we better not do anything sexual because she was more afraid of disobeying God than losing me. She made sure I knew her dealbreakers and I told her mine. She told me if I cheated there would be no talking or reconciliation. Me betraying her like that would simply mean she did not mean as much to me as I meant to her. I knew she meant it and I believed her.

The day I proposed, we were at her house where she was putting the final touches to her art piece. I had overheard her telling her friends she did not want an extravagant proposal but a spontaneous one. "I wouldn't mind being proposed to on a Tuesday at 14:39 or something. I just want it to be me and my future husband, taking in the moment of the new chapter and savouring it." So that is what I did. She always listened to nineties RnB when she worked, so that day I made a playlist which included all her favourites, K-Ci and Jojo, Boys II Men, Mary J Blige, Toni Braxton Joe, Donell Jones and all the men and women who made us believe in love. She sang along, sitting on her stool, splashing different colours on her canvas. I was waiting for Joe Thomas' *No One Else Comes Close* to play so I could propose. She was used to wearing headphones when she worked, but I had hidden them, so she listened to the music on the speaker.

I knelt behind her with the ring in my hand. I was so nervous I did not say anything to her or ask her to turn around. I kept repeating the song while she sang along as always, until it replayed for the sixth time.

"*Hezvo,* what kind of shuffle is this?" she shouted, thinking I was busy on my PlayStation. I remained glued to the floor. "Baaabe!" she called, but I kept quiet, still kneeling, hoping she would turn around soon because my knee was giving way. "Baaabe!" she shouted again. "Where is this fine man of mine?" she said under her breath as she turned and faced me. She froze when she saw me on one knee. She had that look on her face, eyes open wide, stone-faced and holding her breath.

"Chipo, you have been someone I never thought I wanted, but someone I definitely needed. You challenge and push me in so many ways and I– I want that to be the rhythm of our love for the rest of my life. Please, will you make me the happiest man on a Tuesday at 14:39 and marry me?" I was nervous. I looked down at the ring and extended my hand to ask for hers.

"About time!" she screamed as she jumped on me. I dropped the ring and she fell into my arms. We both fell on the floor as my knee gave way. We stayed on the floor and laughed.

"I am going to need you to say it before you trick me out of it," I remarked as I gazed into her eyes.

"Hmm, say what?" she responded, smiling.

"Oh, you are not getting away with this one." I laughed, reaching my arms towards her and started tickling her.

"YES!" she screamed as I tickled her.

"Thank you! Was that so hard to say?" I asked, sitting up to look for the ring.

"I love you Tonderai." She grinned as she moved towards me and knelt in front of me.

"And I love you Chipo."

She leaned over and kissed my forehead, I took her hands and kissed them. "Now, help me look for your ring before I demote you to girlfriend again." We laughed as we scoured the floor for the ring I had got from my mother which would now be hers.

***

Most people talk about the three-year itch, but never the one-year glitch after getting married. We were just off. We were like housemates who shared a bed and the last name. We were not fighting, but we never talked. We could not explain what it was, yet it seemed there was a dark cloud over us. I no longer woke her up with kisses and made her late for work with the long showers we took. She no longer waited for me to get home from work to open the door wearing only lingerie. We became strangers and barely spoke. We were in a monotonous place. We both yearned for each other, but no one knew how to initiate the conversation or make the first move. She began to paint more and spent most of the day in her in-house studio. I started working late more and that is how it started.

Her name was Tsungai and she was my secretary. She reminded me of the Chipo I fell for, the Chipo who never missed a chance to make a joke and leave me speechless. For three months, I emotionally cheated on Chipo with Tsungai.

Chipo had begun to bother me. She appeared to be more forgetful, disoriented and always complained about being tired. She would spend the whole day in bed, unaware of the time or date she woke up.

One day when I came from work, I decided to tell her about Tsungai. I had meant to tell her sooner, but there was never the right moment. She looked at me for a long time and I saw the disappointment in her eyes. I began to cry.

"Why?" was the only word that came out of her mouth.

"Chipo, I love you ver…" I blurted, walking towards her. She had grown thinner than I remembered.

"No. That is not what I asked you. *Ndati* why?" she snapped, walking away from me.

"Baby, we were not talking. I was lonely and I– I am so sorry." I begged. I was disgusted with myself. How had I got here? How had I become the person who hurt the person I vowed to protect.

"So, you were lonely and decided to get attention elsewhere? Do you think I wasn't lonely too? You think I didn't miss you and yearn for you?" she said, standing further from me.

"Chipo, I ended it and we can work this out. We can work on us," I pleaded. I felt my eyes stinging. I was going to lose my wife.

"Tonderai, you remember two years ago when you asked me to be your girlfriend? What did I tell you?" she asked sternly.

"Chipo please, we are marrie–"

"So? Do you think us being married will make this invalid?"

I do not know why I had brought our marital status up, but it had made sense at that moment. She began to cry. I wanted to hold her, but I knew I was the last person she wanted to be close to. She began to sob so hard I felt my heart ache. I felt helpless and the only thing I could think of was to get her a glass of water. I hate myself for this part because when I came back, she was lying on the floor, unconscious. I ran over to her and shook her. She did not wake up.

Knowing the terrible medical service in Zimbabwe, I did not bother calling the ambulance. I carried her to my car and drove her to the hospital. I shouted for help as I rushed through the hospital doors, with her lying limp in my arms. The nurses took her from my arms and laid her on a stretcher, which they wheeled into a room I was not allowed to enter. I stayed in the waiting area, pacing up and down. I was confused and afraid. Was I going to lose her twice? I had caused all this and killed the woman I love.

"Mr Tonderai Moyo?" a man wearing a white coat called as he approached the waiting area.

"Yes!" I jolted. He turned towards me.

"Your wife is conscious now, but we have made her as comfortable as best we can. However, I am afraid her tumour has advanced and is inoperable. We would suggest you prepar–"

"Wait. What tumour?" Had he mixed up his patients or were there two Chipo Moyo's? It made no sense because Chipo had never informed me. Why did she not tell me?

"Yes, sir. I am afraid she does not have long. On our last appointment, we had suggested treatment, but her tumour seems to be growing quicker than we expected." He explained it so calmly, I wanted to shake him so he would see how this made no sense to me.

"Appointment? Wait, whe– when was this?"

"The appointment? Uhm, about two months ago. She had declined treatment anyway. She said something about everything falling apart and being betrayed. We believed she was talking about her brain betraying her but we cou– "

"She knew?" She had known about Tsungai but not once did she mention or say anything. But why?

"If you would like to see her, I can take you to her room now," he said, gesturing his hand to lead me to her room. Everything felt louder and brighter. How was I going to face her now? I had cheated on my wife when she needed me the most. How had I not been able to tell she was sick? Her sleeping too much, being a bit disoriented and fatigued was not because she was in a "rut." My wife was suffering from a tumour and her beautiful mind that I had fallen for and loved so very much, was wasting away.

When I got to her room, I saw her holding a clump of her hair. She was cutting it off and putting it in a bag that was on her lap. I softly knocked on the door. She looked up, looked at me and continued cutting her hair. I walked into the room. The smell brought bad memories I had fought to stash at the back of my mind. Each tube that was connected to her and the white covers that shielded her now bony frame, took me back to ten years ago when I lost my mother to cancer. My initial instinct was to run away and leave the building, not because of her, but because of the building I had avoided for as long as I could remember. I gathered all the courage I could find in my being and walked in. I did not know if I should sit or stand, which she probably did not take notice of because she was looking at herself in a hand mirror. I stood beside her, but she ignored me. I knelt beside her bed and reached for her hand. She pushed me away.

"W-why didn't you tell me?" I asked her, my eyes itching with tears again. She looked different. Her big bright eyes were now hollow; her once ample flesh I loved to touch each morning had been replaced by a bony frame I could not recognise. And her hair, the hair I loved to run my hands through when I kissed her, was no more. Only patches and bald spots. I wept.

"Would you have stopped cheating?" she asked me so calmly. I could not tell if she was angry or not. She tied the bag with the hair and handed it to the nurse.

"I am sorry, I– I am so sor… Tell me how I can fix this, please," I begged her, kneeling beside her. I was not doing this to manipulate her to forgive me. I meant it with every ounce of my being.

"I am dying, Tonderai. What is there to fix?" Her demeanour was so calm whilst I was in shambles. I did not want her to bear my mistak– my choice, but I am sure it played a part in her tumour growing so fast.

"I am sorry. I didn't know you were so si–"

"Please, don't."

"Are you going to leave me? I understand if you do because I do not deserve y– "

"I am dying Tonderai. Whether I stay or leave, I am dying." Each time she said dying, my heart dropped. It was dawning on me that I was losing my wife. I was going to lose the person who had been by my side and who had taught me so much. I was going to lose her twice, first as a wife and then eternally. She lay on the bed and turned to face the wall. I was still kneeling beside her.

"Can I stay with you here?"

She did not reply, but I stayed. I brought the chair next to the bed and sat there, staring at her and watching her chest go up and down slowly. When she started snoring softly like she always did when she was deep in sleep, I reached for her hand and touched it. I looked at the veins that ran across it and I noticed she no longer wore her wedding ring. How had I missed that?

I took in every inch of her face; her beautiful skin, the once long and bouncy curls that were now patches on her oval shaped head. I traced her nose which I kissed each morning before she woke up, the full lips which produced malicious words when her brilliant brain could not solve a problem or when I could not understand what she meant, even after she had explained it to me numerous times, the lips I loved to kiss, the ones that uttered I love you first before I was ready to say it.

They say you never miss a good thing till it's gone, but what do you do when it is within reach, and see it slipping away? I looked at her, breathing softly, connected to different tubes and barely looking like herself. I had so many things I wanted to say, so many wrongs I wanted to make right. I believed her when she said if I cheated there would be no talking or reconciliation, which is why I was not surprised when the nurse woke me up a few hours later and told me my wife was dead.

THE END.

Glossary

SHONA

1. Sadza - Zimbabwe's food staple, a thick porridge made from finely ground white maize
2. Varungu- white people
3. Muzukuru - grandchild
4. Kunyepa - lies/ you are lying
5. Ruware - an area of bare rock with slightly domed profile
6. Hunza - bring/ give me
7. Kuno - here
8. Zigwara - you coward
9. Econet - telecommunications service provider in Zimbabwe
10. NetOne - telecommunications service provider in Zimbabwe
11. Telecel - telecommunications service provider in Zimbabwe
12. Mukoma - older brother
13. Ambuya - older woman (in context)
14. Tora - take
15. Imi - you (they form)

16. Amai - mother
17. Iwe - you (singular form)
18. Nyarai - have shame
19. Shuwa - sure
20. Dzikama - calm down
21. Roora - bride price
22. Newe - with you
23. N'anga - traditional healer
24. Huyai - come
25. Svikai - arrive
26. Taurai - speak/talk
27. Shumba - lion
28. Sabhuku - village headman
29. Hozi - bedroom
30. Nhava - pouch
31. Njuga - poker
32. Gota - the boys' bedroom
33. Matohwe - snot apple
34. Man'a - cracked heels
35. Zvakanaka - all is well
36. Mwanangu - my child
37. Mhapa - leather dress cloth that is worn to cover the fore part of the body
38. Shashiko - leather dress cloth that is worn to cover

the back

39. Munondinyaudzirei - why do you make noise/ disturb me
40. Pangu ndapedza - I have done my part
41. Varume - men
42. Mwari wangu - my God
43. Chii chaitika? - what happened?
44. Vawira - she fell (in context)
45. Maswera sei? - how was your day / good evening
46. Handiti? - right?
47. Muka - wake up
48. Hangu - used to downplay what one has done
49. Wanzwa? - did you hear me? (in context)
50. Hezvo - wow
51. Kombi - a commuter omnibus
52. Hameni - amen
53. Ndati - I said
54. Pasara ini - I am the only one left
55. Madzimai eruwadzano - ladies church group
56. Akandipa - they gave me
57. Sisi - sister
58. Mudiwa - my love
59. Dzangaradzimu - tall apparition
60. Ndamhanya - I ran

61. Chinyarara mwana - hush child
62. Kwete - no
63. Kwakanaka? - is everything alright?
64. Pafunge - think about it
65. Saka? - so?
66. Toita sei? - what shall we do?
67. Chikendikeke - candy cake
68. Handei - let's go
69. Maflawu - a kid's ball game
70. Simuka - stand up
71. Pamushana - a place in the sun
72. Asi ziva kuti handisi kusara - but know I am not being left behind
73. Maita - thank you
74. Achinjanja - a totem
75. Mukwasha - son in law
76. Raka raka - a kid's game
77. Hamusi kunditeerera - you are not listening to me
78. Ndamuziva - I know them
79. Wandiruma - you bit me
80. Urikutii? - what are you saying?
81. Pamusoroi - excuse me
82. Amai - mother
83. Iwe todzizivirepi mota dzakadai? - where would we

know such beautiful cars?

84. Kutoita misangano - holding meetings
85. Pfutseke - go away
86. Sendiraini - sanitary line
87. Rovambira - black mamba

NDEBELE

1. Tokoloshi - goblin
2. Vele - just
3. Woza - come
4. Haibo - no
5. Makoti - daughter in law
6. Nkosi yami - my God
7. Nkhulu - grandfather
8. Gogo - grandmother
9. Sthandwa sami - my love
10. Indodakadzi - daughter
11. Isitshwala - Zimbabwe's food staple, a thick porridge made from finely ground white maize
12. Amasi - fermented milk
13. Litshonile njani? - how are you?
14. Yebo - yes
15. Umfana wami - my boy
16. Kodwa - but

Acknowledgements

I would like to Thank God first and foremost for the gift of making things up and making people "believe" them. I am forever grateful for that.

Thank you to my editors, Rumbidzai Samantha Vazhure and Lazarus Panashe Nyagwambo and Daniel Mutendi for your great feedback; I appreciate your constructive criticism and valuable time.

I would love to thank my friends and family for their support while I worked on this anthology. And lastly, I would love to say thank you to my younger self for pushing me to finally publish my work.

To my readers, thank you for purchasing, reading and supporting my writing and my YouTube channel: What's Rudo Reading?

RUDO DIANA MAZVITA MANYERE grew up in Zimbabwe. Her first literary contribution was three short stories to the Brilliance of Hope, an anthology of short stories compiled by Samantha R. Vazhure (of which two are included in this collection). She has written articles for 263 Africa Magazine and is a reviewer of African literature.

She is a bookstagrammer and booktuber who reviews African Literature on her Youtube channel, What's Rudo

Reading? and won the 2021 Afrobloggers Reviewer of the year. Rudo is also part of Tandem Collectives and is among a group of black women and marginalised groups who read and review books written by white people about black people to make sure they are correctly represented.

www.ingramcontent.com/pod-product-compliance
Lightning Source LLC
Chambersburg PA
CBHW010356310726
48979CB00006B/1060

* 9 7 8 1 9 1 4 2 8 7 2 6 8 *